For fourteen years now *Perry Rhodan* has been acknowledged to be the world's top-selling science fiction series. Originally published in magazine form in Germany, the series has now appeared in hardback and paperback in the States.

Over five hundred *Perry Rhodan* clubs exist on the Continent and *Perry Rhodan* fan conventions are held annually. The first Perry Rhodan film, *SOS From Outer Space*, has now been released in Europe.

The series has sold over 140 million copies in Europe alone.

D1579564

Also available in the *Perry Rhodan* series

Kurt Mahr

PERRY RHODAN 18:

Menace of the Mutant Master

Futura Publications Limited
An Orbit Book

An Orbit Book

First published in Great Britain in 1976
by Futura Publications Limited
Copyright © 1972 by Ace Books
An Ace Book, by arrangement with
Arthur Moewig Verlag
Apollo Murdered © 1972 by Ray Bradbury;
by permission of the author
Death Rides the Spaceways (Scientifilm World)
© 1954 by Authentic Science Fiction; by permission
of the author
When the Marsboy's Time Came copyrighted as
Native Son by Greenleaf Publishing Co, 1953;
by arrangement with the author's agent
Pursuit to Mars, originally copyrighted as
Edison's Conquest of Mars; revised and edited
version copyrighted 1969, 1972 by Forrest J Ackerman

DEDICATION
This English Edition is dedicated to
(quite naturally) the Master Mind of Nexialist Fiction
A E 'SLAN' VOGT

ISBN 0 8600 7917 1
Printed in Great Britain by
Richard Clay (The Chaucer Press), Ltd.,
Bungay, Suffolk
Futura Publications Limited,
110 Warner Road, Camberwell, London SE5

1 / THE IMPOSSIBLE EXPLOSIONS

Great risk always accompanied Perry Rhodan on his missions in space.

One day he might be the victim of a crippling accident. Even a killing one.

Or meet his master.

Then Col. Freyt would have to *try* to fill his spacesuit.

So the colonel smiled as he spoke the words, 'The boss's arrival is scheduled for shortly after midnight,' and his relief that Rhodan was coming back was evident to his adjutant. Terrania, the Gobi base of the New Power, would breathe easier with its leader safely back.

Freyt was convinced that the survival of the artificial political structure known as the New Power was dependent on Perry Rhodan's continued existence. And much more: the welfare of the entire human race. Which was why Freyt was rejoicing that Rhodan had emerged once again safe and sound from one of his interplanetary adventures and was now on his way back to Earth.

'No official reception, as usual, I suppose?' ventured the adjutant.

'As usual,' confirmed the colonel.

Terrania, the capital of the New Power, established

in the heart of the great Gobi desert, was a city in growth. It currently numbered half a million inhabitants.

Science had transformed the climate. Artificial rainfall, produced according to need, changed 15,000 square miles of hilly desert country into an ever green and flowering garden. Terrania was indisputably one of the most beautiful cities of the world.

In the immediate vicinity of the metropolis rose the shining energy dome which housed and protected the actual center of the New Power. The vibrations of the dome would ward off any hostile attempt to approach the heart of the new city.

Shortly after midnight, in anticipation of Rhodan's arrival, Freyt and his adjutant left the administration building and the energy barrier.

The colonel and his aide walked along the outskirts of the city and saw the flat buildings at the edge of the rocketport loom up in the dim light of the stars.

A bright light suddenly skittered across the landing area. Puzzled, Freyt stopped in his tracks, looked around. 'What was that?'

Another lightning flash, this time from far beyond the roofs of Terrania, and almost simultaneously there arrived the roaring thunder of an explosion.

Freyt stood stock still. His eyes widened in frightened confusion, failing to comprehend what was going on when the roar of the second explosion swept over them.

'It's over at the salt lake!' he groaned. 'At the reactor installations!'

6

He turned and sped back to the city. The adjutant was running close behind him. They had hardly advanced 30 yards when the thin wail of the alarm sirens reached them.

Still running, Freyt ordered a car via the small sender and receiver set which was standard equipment for his uniform. The car met up with them as they were almost at one of the wide main roads leading into the city.

'What's going on?' asked Freyt, flopping down in the seat next to the driver of the car.

'An explosion in block G, sir!' answered the chauffeur. 'No details are known so far.'

'Please drive me there!' ordered Freyt.

They made a U-turn and the car took off at high speed. With blaring sirens they made sure nothing would obstruct their way. The driver was a real daredevil but Freyt was too preoccupied with other things to pay attention to him.

What the blazes was there in the reactor installation that could be made to explode? Freyt was a soldier first and a technician next but he had a definite idea how a reactor worked. He also knew what kind of materials were used for the construction of a reactor. But try as he might he couldn't think of anything that might have brought about two explosions of the kind they had just heard.

And how was it possible such explosions could even occur in view of the extensive security measures in force there?

Freyt could find no answer to either of his questions. The chauffeur drove the car to the entrance gate of block G where he came to a halt. Freyt was startled out of his thoughts.

Before the two explosions, block G had consisted of a long, low hall in which various separate components, brought in from the outside, were assembled, the end product being the catalyst R reactors. Some 300 men worked there during the day.

Now the outlines of the former assembly hall could still be recognized but otherwise it gave the appearance of a battlefield that had been bombarded for hours by steady gunfire.

Rescue teams had arrived shortly before Freyt. Dressed in protective clothing, the men stomped through the heat of the area which was strewn with debris. They were searching for survivors. From a police inspector Freyt learned that at the time of the explosion about 10 men of the night crew and guards had been present in the building.

Nobody knew anything about the cause of the explosion. With the help of special instruments they had found two spots within the area of block G whose current temperature was over 3600° Fahrenheit. In all likelihood this was where the explosions had taken place.

Freyt turned to the police inspector. 'Have you checked for radioactivity?' he asked.

The police inspector put on a forced smile. 'I beg your pardon, sir! There wasn't a single speck of radioactive material in the whole place!'

Freyt shook his head. 'I want to make sure in any case,' he answered skeptically. 'Call the dosimeter crew!'

The police inspector walked over to his car to pass on the request.

Freyt began to feel ill at ease. 'There's nothing we can do for the time being,' he told his adjutant. 'We'll have to wait till at least the first check has been made.' In the midst of all the excitement he had forgotten all about Rhodan and his impending arrival.

This incident was not just another accident: one of the most important factories had been destroyed. Without the Arkonide reactors there would be no nuclear drive engines—without power units no space-ships—without spacecraft no protection for Earth.

Was it by chance that of all things block G should have fallen victim to the first major accident inside the area of the New Power?

Colonel Freyt began to wonder what chances a sabo-teur would have of getting inside the domain of the New Power, and in case he did get this far how much chance would he have of actually carrying out an act of sabotage?

None whatsoever, was Colonel Freyt's conclusion.

Still, this thought was no comfort to him now.

Freyt looked around, wishing to see the police in-spector and find out from him what in the meantime the result of their search for survivors and traces of radioactivity had been.

He had been so lost in his thoughts that he had failed to notice the arrival of the dosimeter group, all dressed in bright red uniforms, who meanwhile had spread out all over the devastated terrain.

But he couldn't avoid noticing the ear-rending zeeep —zeeep—zeeep of the radiation alarm. The radiation crew had activated their sirens atop the roof of their trucks. Freyt saw that the rescue team began fleeing abruptly from the heap of ruins.

One of the men in the bright red protective uniform approached him. He saluted him hastily and blurted out: 'Emergency, sir! Highest danger. The entire area is contaminated, at least 10 roentgen per hour!'

This was the moment that Freyt changed his opinion about the absolute efficacy of the anti-sabotage safety measures. For a second he lost his composure but regained it instantaneously, his cool reasoning mind winning out. 'What radioactive material?' he asked sharply.

The dosimeter man shook his head. 'We don't know yet; it'll take another 15 minutes to find out.'

'Okay. Let me know as soon as you get the result!'

The man in the bright red uniform saluted. Freyt turned away and marched off. He paid no attention to whether his adjutant was following him. Not until they were both sitting in the car next to each other did he become aware of him again. 'What do you think of this whole affair?' he asked with a grim expression.

'What's the use guessing as long as we have no clues, sir?'

This seemed to make sense. Freyt nodded his head as if to say, you're right!

The whole incident made Freyt feel depressed. It had taken place during the time he had acted as substitute in Terrania during Rhodan's absence. And although it was quite obvious that he personally had had no influence either way in aggravating or easing the catastrophe, he nevertheless felt responsible for it. The fact that the accident had occured during his term of office was interpreted by him as a personal failure.

Another warning signal came painfully loud over the car's radio. 'Stop the car!' shouted Freyt.

The car came to a sudden halt. Freyt was hurled forward and hit his head against the windshield but paid no attention to it. He concentrated on the announcement: 'Three recently completed ships of the Z fleet, so called space destroyers, took off a few minutes ago without starting clearance. The identities of the pilots aboard are unknown. The ships almost immediately reached top speed and have already passed beyond the local radar range.

'Calling Colonel Freyt! Calling Colonel Freyt! ...'

Freyt gritted his teeth. He flipped on the switch of the telecom sender. The small screen came alive showing the grim face of the man who was giving the alarm.

'This is Freyt speaking! What's the matter?'

Freyt noticed how the man switched off all sender channels except his own. 'Three destroyers have been kidnapped, sir!' he reported curtly.

'Kidnapped!' growled Freyt. 'How on earth can a destroyer be kidnapped?'

The answer was immediate if unsatisfactory. 'We've no idea, sir, how this could have happened. Our robot guards functioned in the usual manner, we know that for sure. None of the robots noticed anybody or anything attempting to approach these three destroyers.'

Freyt stared straight ahead. 'Who's conducting the investigation?' he asked shortly.

'Major de Casa, sir.'

Freyt shook his head wearily. 'Over and out.'

He ordered his driver to proceed at once to the field where the destroyers were kept. He drove to an area near the immense final assembly halls located in the southern part of the city. These class Z destroyers had been designed by Perry Rhodan himself, based on the original design of the one-seater space fighters which Rhodan had found many years ago in the underground hangars of the ancient Arkonidian Venus base. They couldn't properly be called spaceships since they lacked the hyper drive. Their corpuscular-drive engines merely enabled them to accelerate within an extremely short time to the speed of light. However, they were incapable of escaping into the outer reaches of space via a hyper-space jump.

Nevertheless, these Z ships were at least 500 years ahead of anything that the most modern techniques on Earth could produce. They were a potentially fearful weapon in the hands of those who knew how to handle them.

While the car was speeding south to the assembly halls Freyt issued a series of commands. The defense corps was intructed to shoot immediately and without warning at any plane trying to take off from Terrania. Hand in hand with this order followed another command grounding all air vehicles. And finally, a large number of robot guards were sent inside all spaceships to prevent any unauthorized take-off.

There were more important things to lose than these three destroyers. There was so much more at stake. Freyt broke out in a cold sweat wondering what might have happened if the unknown abductors had managed to steal the two cruisers of the new Terra class—space-spheres with a diameter of nearly 600 feet, armed with the most sophisticated weapons and capable of executing instantaneous hyper-transitions throughout the universe.

In the meantime, however, the little red warning lights were blinking regularly and calmly from atop the gigantic spacespheres stationed on their launching pads.

The car stopped in front of the heavy, shining figure of a robot that barred the way leading to the area where the three kidnapped destroyers had been standing. Freyt motioned to the robot to step closer, then looked at it. The robot registered the brain-wave pattern of the colonel and raised his hand in salute.

The car started up again and drove another 150 feet till it came to a halt once more before a group of men who were engaged in an animated discussion. Freyt got out of the car.

Major de Casa stepped over to Freyt. His face showed clearly the effect that the sudden disappearance of the three ships had had on him: surprise, disbelief ... and some fear.

'How did it all happen?' asked Freyt.

'There are no eye-witnesses except for our robots, sir,' answered de Casa readily, obviously relieved that somebody would now take charge of the whole affair. 'All we know is what the robots told us, and that was very little indeed. They reported they walked up and down their assigned route. The area is absolutely flat and unobstructed. Their infra-red eyes could have spotted even a tiny mouse trying to approach the destroyers.

'But neither man nor mouse nor anything else had been seen by them. All they noticed was the destroyers suddenly beginning to lift off the ground, then vanishing at top speed. The incident was reported at once to the command center but before anyone there could react and undertake any counter measures not a trace of the destroyers could be found.'

'What course were they flying when they took off?' asked Freyt.

'Southeast, sir.'

Freyt looked attentively at the major. 'Any conclusion one might draw from this?' he wanted to know.

De Casa smiled. 'Most likely that we should not try looking for the unknown in that direction.'

Freyt nodded in agreement. 'Probably so.'

Together with de Casa he marched once around the area where the three destroyers had been standing. De Casa had made sure beforehand that the radioactive traces remaining from the starting thrust of the rockets had become minimal and harmless.

No traces were to be seen except for the three burnt-over glassy spots which the engines had left behind after they had started. There were no footprints, no tire tracks—nothing!

Freyt sighed as he returned to his adjutant. 'We don't have even the slightest hint here whether we're dealing with human beings or intelligent extraterrestrial life forms.'

At this instant the driver of the car that had brought

them to the airfield stuck his head out of the window. 'A call for Colonel Freyt!' he shouted.

Freyt took the telecom-receiver the man handed him through the window and saw on the screen a man dressed in the protective suit of the dosimeter crew.

'We've pinpointed the sources of the radiation,' he stated calmly, 'and measured them. Both places with the highest temperatures are also the spots with the most intense radiation, five hundred roentgen per hour each at their center. The radiation consists of beta-minus with about 1.8 and 1.6 MeV, of beta-plus with ...'

'Tell me the elements, will you!' interrupted Freyt impatiently.

'Magnesium-27 and zircon-87, sir.'

Freyt was confused. 'What conclusions can you draw from this?' he asked.

The radiation expert looked annoyed. 'None, sir!' he said. 'Neither magnesium-27 nor zircon-87 belong to the fission products given off during uranium or plutonium fission. We know of no nuclear reaction in connection with these two explosions which would produce these two isotopes.'

Perry Rhodan landed amidst all this confusion.

He realized something unusual must have happened when Colonel Freyt failed to meet him at the landing strip. He ordered one of the all-purpose vehicles to be lowered to the ground from aboard the 180 foot high spacesphere. Then he together with his friend Reginald Bell drove over to the glowing dome of protective energy.

Bell kept peering intently through the windshield. 'What's going on there?' he asked.

Rhodan didn't reply. The automatic barrier registered his mental radiation and the dimensions of the arriving vehicle. A sector opened for a few moments, just large enough to let the car with its occupants pass through the shimmering wall of the energy screen.

The car plunged ahead. Rhodan and Bell got out in front of the tall administration building. A few minutes later they were standing in Freyt's office.

Freyt made no attempt to apologize for his failure to meet them at the landing field. He made his report, precise and grim.

'That's serious,' said Rhodan after having listened to Freyt's account. 'Still, Freyt, you shouldn't blame yourself for what's taken place. We seem to be dealing here with somebody who has a few more tricks up his sleeve than we do.'

'I'm glad you think so, sir,' answered Freyt. 'Nevertheless ...'

Rhodan waved his hand in protest. 'No nevertheless, Freyt! We'll soon find out what's at the bottom of all of this.'

Freyt cleared his throat. 'Do you think ... perhaps ... extraterrestrial enemies, sir?' he asked.

Rhodan looked at him in surprise. 'Extraterrestrial? No. We couldn't possibly have missed their approach to the airfield.'

Freyt had been thinking about this probability, even before Rhodan had landed. He wasn't sure but what an enemy who could seize unnoticed three destroyers couldn't also have approached Earth unnoticed.

But he kept silent about his thoughts. He knew there was nothing better he could do in such a case than to leave such problems for Perry Rhodan to solve.

Rhodan was taking stock of the situation. All reports transmitted by both search details who were scouring the area of block G and the place where the three destroyers had been stationed, were gathered in his command center, transferred to impulse-strips and then fed to the positronic brain for evaluation.

The positronicon handled this task in its own way. It found 2500 different possible explanations for the explosion in block G and 3800 for the kidnapped destroyers.

Rhodan eliminated of these 6300 possible explanations all but 100 that showed more than a certain degree of probability.

The 100 possibilities were then fed into the deductor combinatoric phase and some answers obtained which greatly resembled those he had meanwhile puzzled out on his own. Khrest assisted him with the last evaluation.

Khrest was the tall, white-haired scientist, one of the two survivors of an Arkonide research expedition which had made an emergency landing on the Moon and had subsequently been destroyed by terrestrial fusion bombs. Khrest was the alien who—quite in contrast to the other survivor, Thora, the female commander of the Arkonide research cruiser—had from the very first sided unconditionally with Rhodan and had had placed at the Earthman's disposal not only the superior means of Arkonide technology but had also transmitted via hypno-schooling the far superior treasure of Arkonide knowledge. Thus Khrest had been instrumental in helping Rhodan to form the New Power and save the world from total destruction by an atomic war.

There was a strange bond of friendship between Khrest and Rhodan. An outsider might observe them for days on end without noticing anything the two had in common. But in times of crises, or impending danger, he would sense the instantaneous accord between them, both agreeing on the necessary course of action without even having to consult each other, for it was based on the highest degree of insight that ever had been reached by intelligent life within the known realm of the galaxy.

Throughout the years, Khrest had come to take part in Earth's development in almost as interested a manner as Rhodan himself, although from a different point of view. The amazing events of the preceding night excited him to the same degree as Rhodan.

'Any idea what might be behind all this?' Khrest inquired of Rhodan.

'No use guessing as long as the positronicon is still busy evaluating.'

'Oh, don't pretend you haven't come to some conclusions of your own, Perry, as to who blew up block G and kidnapped the three destroyers!'

For awhile Rhodan pretended not to have listened to Khrest's remark but then he lifted his head and looked at the Arkonide scientist. 'Oh, sure,' he admitted, 'I have some idea!'

* * *

The positronic evaluation confirmed what Rhodan had surmised.

For reasons obvious to anyone at once when looking at the results of the calculations, Rhodan informed only his closest collaborators. Besides Reginald Bell, Colonel Freyt and Majors Deringhouse and Nyssen, only the Arkonides Khrest and Thora were present at the short briefing session. Khrest looked worried, while Thora was as self-confident as ever, her face radiating unearthly beauty which had not been diminished by the terror-filled days of her latest adventure when she had fled to Venus.

Rhodan placed a pile of thin impulse foils on the table at which the small group was seated. Rhodan's face displayed a serious mood. 'Although more than several thousand explanations had been given by the positronicon for the events of last night,' he began, 'and although we had to eliminate all but those with the greatest degree of probability, we cannot doubt the result of the brain's evaluation.

'The catastrophe in block G which cost 10 human lives, and the abduction of the three newly-constructed destroyers, was not the act of some extraterrestrial enemies. It is a fact, to the best of our knowledge, that no alien intruders can come anywhere near our solar system without being detected in time. This doesn't at all exclude the possibility that some race of far superior intelligence might have played some part in this attack. But this alternative has only a very limited degree of likelihood.

'Therefore we assume this attack was the work of some Earthly foe. The question how both plots could be carried out successfully can be answered logically only in one way: Somebody has arrived at the same solution as we ourselves when we searched out and selected the best qualified type of persons to become our collaborators!'

None of those present, except for Khrest who already knew the result, understood what Rhodan was alluding to.

But then all of a sudden it became clear to them and they also understood why none of the mutants had been invited to this conference. This was in contrast to the usual proceedings. The mutants, to whose special talents a great deal of the New Power's successes were due, had always been previously included in meetings of this kind.

This conference between Rhodan and his inner circle of coworkers took place on the morning of July 20. Almost exactly five years previous to that day the following event had occurred in Gardiner, a small town in Montana near the Wyoming border:

A man had come to Gardiner a few days before. He did not make a very sympathetic impression, although he looked quite prosperous. There were two hotels in Gardiner and he lived in the more expensive of the two.

People in Gardiner were curious by nature. Gardiner was not a tourist center although it was located near the entrance of Yellowstone National Park. Strangers were an unusual sight in the little town and people started to get interested in this visitor.

His name turned out to be Monterny and he was a

natural scientist by profession. Monterny was not especially tall but he was quite heavy. His mighty, hairless head with the deepset eyes led to the simple and plausible conclusion that there was sufficient brain matter inside this skull to make its owner an outstanding scientist.

This was all the information that the good people of Gardiner managed to obtain about that stranger, yet there was one thing they failed to find out: the purpose of Monterny's visit to their little town.

All day long he did nothing but go for walks. Gardiner consisted mostly of one long main street, lined on both sides with one-story houses, inhabited by some 200 persons. There were hardly any side streets. Therefore it seemed to make little sense that the stranger kept roaming up and down Main Street. This led to the rumor that Monterny was waiting for someone.

Monterny did not fail to notice the curious attention he received from all sides. The business that had brought him to this town could do very well without all this curiosity and Monterny started getting nervous when finally, on the 18th of July, he found what he had been seeking.

It was in the late afternoon. He was walking up and down Main Street, as he had been doing for days, when suddenly he noticed a young man driving up to the drugstore in an old jalopy. He stopped and got out of his car, intending to go to the store to buy something.

Monterny was standing on the other side of the street and observed the young man with great interest.

The young fellow, however, was unaware of this. He entered the drugstore. Monterny crossed the street and stood waiting in front of the store.

When the young man came out again, Monterny addressed him: 'Pardon me, could I ask you for a favor?'

The young fellow seemed a bit puzzled. 'What do you want?'

Monterny smiled somewhat embarrassed. 'It's something I'd rather not discuss here in the street. I'm living at Wolfrey's Hotel, would you mind accompanying me there?'

The young fellow was just about to refuse politely when Monterny continued: 'Maybe you could drive me there in your car?'

This was of course utterly ridiculous, for the hotel was just a block away from the drugstore. But somehow Monterny seemed to have found the right approach, for the boy felt flattered that anybody should want to drive in his old jalopy. 'I'll make it worth your while, I promise you,' added Monterny.

Any argument that the young fellow had wanted to advance suddenly seemed to vanish. 'I'll be glad to go with you. Get in, sir!'

They drove to Wolfrey's Hotel and went straight to Monterny's room. 'Sit down, will you!' Monterny said, pointing to a chair, not quite as friendly as he had been before.

The young man took the seat and Monterny sat down opposite him. He stared intently at the young fellow. For awhile the boy looked back in Monterny's eyes, first with a smile, then grinning, finally grimacing stubbornly. Then he averted his eyes and looked around the room, trying to avoid Monterny's glance. The whole thing impressed him as being rather silly. Then Monterny began to speak: 'Have you ever seen me before?'

The young fellow was puzzled and replied: 'No. I've been away for two weeks. I've stayed with some friends in ...'

'Idaho Falls!' interrupted Monterny. 'That's right, isn't it?'

The boy wasn't especially surprised. 'That's right. How do you know that? Did you ask my parents?'

Monterny shook his head. 'No. I've never laid eyes on your parents! Your name is Ted McMurray and your friends call you "Tiger" because you like to wear jackets with a tiger pattern. You have friends in Idaho Falls because you used to live there with your parents. Your father is a nuclear reactor technician who was exposed to some radiation during an accident. He was pensioned off because of his injuries. You were born about one year after that nuclear accident.

'Two days ago when you were in Idaho Falls you met two girls, Sue and Dorothy. You can't make up your mind which one you like best. That's right, isn't it?'

McMurray jumped to his feet. After Monterny's first words he had wanted to protest against the familiar tone with which the stranger was addressing him; but then he had felt increasingly perplexed at all that man was telling him about himself. Most of the things were of course not too difficult to find out. Almost anybody could do it if they would set their mind to it.

But that he had met these two girls in Idaho Falls and that things had gone pretty far between him and Sue and Dorothy, wasn't known to a living soul—neither he nor the girls would ever talk about it.

'How come ... How do you ...?' stammered Ted.

'I know a lot more about you,' said Monterny. 'To be exact: I know as much about you as you yourself. And in particular I know of something you have never discussed with anybody. You have a special gift which is almost unique in the world.'

Ted turned pale and fell back into his chair. His eyes had a dangerous glitter as he asked Monterny: 'What do you want?'

Monterny paid no attention to his question. 'You need only close your eyes and wish you were again in Idaho Falls—and you'd be there, correct? The phenomenon is known as teleportation and you are an outstanding teleportationist. What's the greatest distance you've covered so far?'

'Two hundred ...' answered Ted impulsively but clammed up again at once.

'Miles,' completed Monterny with a smug, satisfied smile. 'That's very good for a beginning but you'll have to improve on that later.'

He stood up and continued while calmly pacing the room: 'Ever since you realized you have this special talent, you've been dreaming that some day you'll become an important man. I'll provide you with that opportunity. You'll work for me—at first for $2000 a month plus expenses, with the sky the limit. Agreed?' He turned around and gazed at Ted.

The boy stood up. 'You're right,' he admitted with a surprisingly firm voice. 'I've been dreaming for years of becoming a great man. But I've always dreamed that I'd accomplish it with everything above board. The offer you just made seems to be a bit shady, otherwise you'd come right out with it to my parents.

'I don't need your two thousand bucks, I don't want your expense account! And what's more, I can't stand the sight of *you*!'

With this Ted turned on his heels and walked out the door. Monterny made no attempt to hold him back. For a few moments he stared, with hate-filled eyes, at the door that had just closed behind Ted Mc-Murray.

Then he shut his eyes and began to concentrate on something.

Meanwhile Ted had stormed out of the hotel. His head was filled with all kinds of confused thoughts. He got into his car, made a U-turn by crossing a double line, intending to drive home.

At this instant a strange force invaded his conscious awareness like a furious blow. The turmoil of confused thoughts suddenly vanished from his brain and Ted knew only one wish:

Return to the stranger!

He backed up to the hotel entrance, got out of his car, passed by the startled Mr. Wolfrey and walked upstairs.

The door to Monterny's room was open. Ted entered without knocking.

Monterny welcomed him with a smile. 'Well done, my boy!'

He carefully studied Ted for several moments. The boy's eyes had a blank, glassy stare, just what Monterny expected to see in someone who had come under his mental spell.

'You'll go back home now to your parents,' commanded Monterny, 'and you'll tell them that I asked you to accompany me to my hotel because I mistook you for someone else. For the next 20 days you'll keep on living the way you've always done. No changes. Except for one thing: you won't make any teleportation jumps and neither will you tell a living soul that you are capable of such things.

'In 20 days, however—remember the date: August 7 at 5 P.M.—you'll come to Salt Lake City by teleportation. Do you know where the big Mormon Temple is?'

Ted nodded silently.

'Fine. I'll be standing in front of the main entrance and wait for you. And don't forget, boy: You can become a great man with my help but I'll always remain boss!'

Twenty days later, as Monterny had ordered, Ted McMurray disappeared from Gardiner never to be seen there again. Nobody made any connection between Ted's disappearance and the stranger who had left Gardiner already 20 days ago.

The police made an investigation and tried to find Ted's whereabouts but to no avail. When finally the police discontinued their search Ted's father died after a long lingering illness caused by the nuclear accident some two decades earlier. The people in Gardiner believed his end had been hastened by grief over his only son's disappearance.

Clifford Monterny meanwhile continued gathering around him people with special gifts. He sought them out in those places where increased cases of radioactive radiation had occurred because he knew that radioactivity will bring about changes in human genes not necessarily always of a negative nature.

Monterny did nothing different than Rhodan had done several years before him: he put together a mutant corps. The only—but significant—difference from Perry Rhodan's procedure in engaging the services of these mutants was that Monterny did not bother asking the members of his mutant corps whether they wanted to work for him or not. All it took for him was a brief meeting of a few seconds' duration to absorb their brain-wave pattern. This enabled him to read his victim's thoughts even when they were separated by thousands of miles from him and to force his will on them without their offering any resistance.

For Monterny was a mutant himself—the most powerful telepath, hypno and suggestor in one person. In this respect he represented an absolutely unique exception.

His involuntary followers called him the Mutant Master. Most of them didn't even know him in person. He realized that he was carrying on a dangerous business and that a small mistake might bring about his downfall.

He was satisfied to know that once someone entered his service they could never escape from his influence. Wherever they might be, he always held them firmly in his power.

Ted McMurray had become his first victim. Five years later Monterny had assembled as many highly efficient mutants as he needed to plan his first attack.

This attack was directed against the man whose mere success had been sufficient cause to arouse Monterny's eternal hatred.

And this man was Perry Rhodan.

2/ GENERAL COSMIC CO. MAKES NEWS

It had taken several days of hard work for Rhodan and Khrest to gather all the material which in their opinion might furnish some clue to the identity of the unknown attacker. They spent hours transposing it to the complicated Arkonide machine code and then fed it to the positronic brain for evaluation.

The result had been very meager.

The positronicomputer claimed that some economic power was behind all the acts of sabotage, kidnapping and aggression which employed economic means to undermine the New Power and bring about its downfall.

The goal of the unknown power was stated simply as: world domination.

'That isn't too helpful, what the positronicon has told us,' sighed Rhodan.

During the past few days the situation had become aggravated. Several scientists who had visited the space academy at Terrania had disappeared over night. Somebody had stolen a series of tiny engine drive components and had made off with them.

The Unknown displayed a great deal of activity. The only people capable of keeping him in check were Rhodan's Mutant Corps since the aggressor himself was working with the help of mutants.

But even mutants couldn't be everywhere at the

same time. To deploy them at the right place and at the right time would have required someone who could guess in advance the plans of the unknown foe.

This was a task that neither Khrest nor Rhodan, and not even the positronic brain, was capable of handling.

Rhodan took care that the necessary information reached the Terranian Defense Federation via secret channels. This mighty worldwide secret service organization was directed by Allen D. Mercant, who had played such an important and positive role during the first few months after the New Power had been established.

Mercant set in motion his extensive machinery for obtaining secret information and already one day later he sent the first clue to Perry Rhodan.

Perry Rhodan regarded this clue as sufficiently important to investigate it more thoroughly in person. A few hours after he had received the news from Mercant, he was on his way to Sacramento, California where according to Mercant's informants a machine factory had begun to place robot-guided agricultural machines on the market.

Rhodan refrained from marching directly into the lion's den. He didn't go to the firm's office right away but rented a room in a hotel. He let a day go by before he got in touch with Mercant's two agents, who were counted among the most able people working for the Terranian Defense Federation. They were Captain Barina and Lieutenant Richman.

Rhodan and Barina met in a cafeteria while Richman was roving through the city keeping his eyes open for any interesting bits of additional information. Barina was a short, fairly stout man, of Italian extraction. 'Splendidly done, sir!' he stated after having made sure that nobody could listen in to their conversation. 'Not a single soul except for Richman has the faintest idea you've come here to Sacramento.'

Rhodan smiled. He had taken special precautionary measures for this trip. Two outstanding make-up men had changed his face so that one would have to be a very sharp observer or have known Rhodan intimately for a long time in order to recognize him. He wore a facial mask but no beard or wig since this seemed to assure him of greater safety and comfort. Rhodan realized that this additional lack of disguise might perhaps present a tiny chance that he might be given away.

Barina had found him first of all because they had arranged to meet in this cafeteria at a certain time and secondly because Rhodan wore as previously agreed a tiny but visible scar above his left eyebrow.

'What's new?' asked Rhodan.

'Nothing,' answered Barina. 'Unfortunately Raleigh is behaving like the most honorable businessman."

'Raleigh?'

'Yes, the owner of Farming Tools and Machines. He's selling his automated ploughs very cheap and out in the open. In the few days since he's started this sale his customers have at least tripled. And the buyers can't praise the merchandise enough!'

'Have you had a closer look from the inside?'

Barina nodded. 'Of course. But I couldn't find anything. We haven't the faintest idea where Raleigh

31

keeps his construction plans and designs. Provided he ...' Barina hesitated.

'Provided he ... ?' Rhodan urged him to continue.

'... has any construction designs somewhere in the factory. Richman found out that Raleigh—or rather his firm—received large shipments a couple of days before the sale began.'

'Where did these shipments originate from?'

'From Salt Lake City.'

'Did you follow up the lead?'

'Not yet, there was no time.'

Rhodan reflected. From the start it had been a mystery—provided there was even any connection between the robot-guided ploughs and the thefts in Terrania—how a simple machine factory, which undoubtedly was not equipped to handle such jobs, could have placed finished products on the market within such a short time.

'Have you ever met Raleigh in person?' asked Rhodan.

'No. But I have on several occasions seen him from fairly close. Makes a pleasant impression at first sight.'

'And how about the second time around?'

Barina made a face. 'Oh, no. He's the smooth type: friendly to your face but sly and devious behind your back.'

Rhodan's plan had all been worked out. 'You'll call on him this afternoon and pretend to be a potential buyer,' he suggested to Barina. 'We'll figure out something that will permit us to find out as much as possible of his way of negotiating and his reactions in general.

'I'll take over for the second half as soon as you've obtained that information.'

'That's fine with me,' replied Barina. 'But how about Richman?'

'He can try in the meantime to track down who the supplier in Salt Lake City is.'

At about the same time the following happened in New York to a very innocuous-looking man whose slightly deformed back gave him a somewhat pitiful appearance:

He was having lunch at a cafeteria. He had carried his tray with a T-bone steak, string beans and French fries to a vacant table and sat down to enjoy his meal. About five minutes later, as he had decided with displeasure that the steak was not as tender as he had hoped it would be, a young man joined him at his table. The young man was tall, handsome and healthy-looking.

'Had bad luck around the corner?' inquired the older man of the new arrival.

'Around the corner' meant the stock exchange on Wall Street around the corner from the cafeteria.

The young man glanced up from his plate and studied the older man for a moment. Then with a sullen look he replied rudely: 'That's none of your business.'

But the older man was not so easily put off. He said gently: 'I have a flair for such things. Maybe I could help you.'

'You?' came the answer in one word which contained all the contempt the young man could put into it.

But the insult didn't seem to deter the older man. He simply nodded and said with a firm voice: 'Yes, me!'

And that was no exaggeration; for the man with the hunchback, the timid, insignificant exterior and the thin crown of faded, blondish-gray hair was Homer G. Adams—officially head of the General Cosmic Company, the largest industrial concern on Earth, and also the Minister for Industry and Finances of the New Power.

'I know a few of those tricks,' continued Adams, toying with a matchbox, 'they use to separate hot-headed greenhorns from their money. And that's why I also know some tricks to help those poor guys get their money back again.'

The young man, a bit embarrassed, picked over his food on his plate. 'Have you ever heard of the deal with Allied Airlines?' he asked.

'Good grief—did you buy any Allied Airline shares?

The young man nodded and said bitterly: 'Yes, four days ago.'

'And how much did you lose?' Adams wanted to know.

'Everything!'

'How much is everything?'

'A bit over $12,000.'

'That's quite a lot of money for a young fellow. What's your name, if I may ask?'

'Elmer Bradley. I'm an industrial draughtsman. I in-

34

herited that money not long ago from an old aunt of mine.'

He stared at Adams as if he expected the little hunchback to introduce himself in turn now.

'My name is Adams,' obliged Adams.

There were countless people by the name of Adams in the USA. There was no reason to assume that anybody would automatically connect him with the General Cosmic Company.

'And what tips could you give me, Mr. Adams?' asked Bradley.

'No tips, young man, but I'm willing to lend you the same sum you've just lost on the stock exchange. I'd like you to have another go at it.'

He'll probably think I'm a bragging old fool, thought Adams with amusement.

Bradley asked: 'Right now?'

Adams shook his head. 'Come to my office when it's convenient for you. I'll let you have the money and at the same time can study the stock market a bit so that you'll know where and what you should buy.'

He took a paper napkin lying on the table and wrote a few lines. Then he pushed the napkin over to Bradley.

'General Cosmic?' Bradley asked surprised. 'Are you perhaps . . . ?'

Adams waved him off with a smile. 'Oh, no. There are at least ten Adams in our firm and not a single one is related to the boss. Will you come?'

Bradley grinned. 'You bet your life!'

*   *   *

Barina made a sullen face. 'Nothing,' he said. 'They have no plough shares capable of driving up a 30% grade hillside slope. They all but laughed in my face when I inquired about such an automatic model.'

'That was the idea,' Rhodan laughed in turn. 'Did you speak with Raleigh?'

'Yes, for almost 20 minutes.'

'And?'

Barina shrugged his shoulders. 'I would say your idea didn't seem to work out.'

Rhodan apparently did not mind. 'In any case I've something else up my sleeve.'

'I'm sure you'll need it,' stated Barina bluntly.

That evening around seven o'clock Rhodan phoned the Farming Tools and Machines.

Raleigh was not particularly pleased about this late call.

'I realize that I'm imposing on your time,' said Rhodan, 'but I absolutely must have a talk with you at once!'

'Anybody can say that!' protested Raleigh. 'Who are you?'

'Somebody who can cause you a lot of trouble unless you'll come to terms with me,' answered Rhodan ominously. He was surprised that Raleigh hadn't hung up on him long since. Could a bad conscience have held him back from doing so?

'Nobody can cause me any difficulties!' claimed Raleigh.

'All the more reason to listen to me, if you really believe that!' countered Rhodan.

36

There was a slight pause, then Raleigh said: 'Alright, come and see me, if you insist!'

'What's the address?' asked Rhodan.

'2035 Parkway Drive—to my home.'

Rhodan made careful preparations for this interview. He was certain that Raleigh would not be able to recognize him because of his facial disguise. In addition he was equipped with a handy pulseray gun and a psychray weapon. These were all the arms he could carry on him. He had even had to dispense with the Arkonide transporter suit which would have protected him from all kinds of weapons, since the strange-looking suit would have given him away right away.

He hoped that it would not be necessary for him to use the psychray. Raleigh most likely was nothing but a relatively unimportant link in the chain of conspiracy against the New Power. It would be advantageous for his investigation if the unknown foe remained in the dark as long as possible whether the counterattack had already begun or not.

He drove out to Parkway Drive in a car he had rented for the duration of his stay in Sacramento. Raleigh lived in a ridiculously old-fashioned, large but undoubtedly very expensive house. A private road led from the street up to his own driveway.

Rhodan arrived at 20 minutes before nine. It was a dark night; the only light came from the distant twinkling stars in the sky. Rhodan looked around trying in vain to spot Barina who was supposed to be hidden somewhere close and waiting for him.

37

Rhodan rang the doorbell. He waited for someone to answer the door.

According to Barina's description it must be Raleigh himself who let him in.

'My name is Wilder,' Rhodan introduced himself. 'I appreciate that you're still seeing me tonight.' He stretched out his hand in greeting but Raleigh overlooked it pointedly.

Rhodan was led into a small room which seemed to be Raleigh's study. Raleigh pointed to a chair without saying a word. Rhodan sat down. 'Well?' asked Raleigh.

Rhodan leaned back comfortably in his chair and crossed his legs. 'You have stolen my invention,' he said casually and with a voice lacking any emphasis.

Raleigh, who had taken a seat behind his writing desk, sat bolt upright at Rhodan's words. He leaned halfway across the top of his writing desk, looking very frightened. 'Your invention ... ?' he gasped. 'Say that again!'

Rhodan smiled accommodatingly and repeated: 'You have stolen my invention.'

Raleigh sank back in his chair. 'Which invention?' He had calmed down very rapidly. *Too fast*, thought Rhodan.

'Don't pretend you don't know,' answered Rhodan. 'For the last 15 years you've been producing harrows, ploughs and some small agricultural machinery—the kind of thing that has been known to man for the last several thousand years. But just a few days ago you brought out for the first time since you founded your firm something radically new—and this is what you've stolen from me!'

Raleigh did not blink an eye. 'Can you prove that?' he encountered.

'Of course. Would you like me to do that in court?'

'I even insist on it,' Raleigh answered with a firm voice.

This was when Rhodan realized that his bluff would not work. Raleigh knew only too well where the robot guidance system of his ploughs had come from. He didn't fall for Rhodan's trick.

'You'll be sorry,' Rhodan tried once more.

Raleigh stood up. '*I* won't be sorry,' he said stiffly, 'but *you* will!'

Rhodan also rose from his chair. With an inconspicuous move he pulled the small psychray from his pocket and pointed it at Raleigh.

Raleigh noticed it at once and sneered at Rhodan with an ugly grin. He was not afraid.

'You'll tell me now who your backers are!' commanded Rhodan. And with these words he depressed the lever of the cerebral weapon and waited for his command to be transported into hypnotic impulses which would force Raleigh to speak.

But Raleigh was still grinning sardonically.

Rhodan realized that things were not proceeding according to the way he had planned them. Why did it take so long for Raleigh to fall under the hypnoray's spell? Or ...

'I thought so,' stated Raleigh cynically. 'What is that thing you're holding in your hand? A hypnotizer?' He laughed mockingly. 'This time you got the wrong person, you ... you ... Rhodan-follower, trying to overthrow the whole world!'

Rhodan felt the blind hatred coming from this man who apparently had not recognized him but who nevertheless had some idea from which camp his late night visitor had come.

But before he could decide what new tactics to pursue both doors leading into Raleigh's study opened wide. Two men stood in the darkened doorway, two on each side, pointing automatic pistols straight at Rhodan. There was no doubt at all what their intentions were.

'Seize him!' hissed Raleigh.

Rhodan didn't give up yet. He knew there was not enough time to reach for his pulseray gun. But he still couldn't believe that not only should Raleigh be impervious to the psychray but that also his men should not respond to its hypnotic suggestion.

Rhodan turned a bit sideways until the effective cone of the hypnotic raybeamer would play on one of the two doors. He ordered: 'Leave me alone! Put your guns down!'

The men did nothing of the sort. They marched side by side into the room and Rhodan heard the steps of the other two men likewise approaching from the other door.

For a tiny fraction of a second Rhodan's analytical mind seemed paralyzed by the thought that his always and unfailing effective hypnoray gun should now not be worth any more than the metal it was made of. But as fast as lightning he overcame this terrible shock and knew that he must use delaying tactics. His foremost task now was to gain time so that Captain Barina would have a chance to intervene in this desperate situation.

'Stop!' shouted Rhodan to the men. 'Another step and I'll reduce you to a little heap of ashes!'

He raised the psychray another inch and ostentatiously placed his finger on the trigger. The men stopped and Rhodan recognized where his chances lay. He must go on talking!

'You're thinking you only need to push down the triggers of your pistols to finish me off, aren't you? Don't forget even if you should hit me I'd be alive long enough to take all of you with me!'

It was just foolish talk, calculated to win time. And it seemed to work, for one of the four guards hesitated and looked questioningly at Raleigh.

Raleigh didn't know what to think of it. But still he shouted to his men: 'He's only bluffing, that thing is a hypno-weapon, he can't shoot with it.'

But his lack of reassurance communicated itself to his men. They didn't move forward. They stood there and stared at Rhodan.

'Well?' growled Rhodan. 'Do you want a taste of it? I promise you the end will be swift and painless!'

One of the four men suddenly threw his head back and yelled: 'He's only bluffing! Don't listen to him!'

Rhodan could see how his finger curled around the trigger and he thought with regret that Barina would be too late if he ever came.

'A marvelous tip, Mr. Adams!' Bradley shouted

with joy. 'Hanson & Sons has gone up 12 points since yesterday!'

Adams was not overtly impressed by Bradley's jubilant outburst. With a slightly mocking smile he replied: 'Just be patient! They'll keep going up. I estimate another 30 points at least.'

Bradley sat down opposite Adams. In the past three days he had visited the old man twice a day. Adams received him in a small office which in no way revealed anything about who he was in reality.

He had asked himself repeatedly what would cause him to have taken such a fancy to this young man. But he could not find any satisfactory explanation. He simply liked Elmer Bradley.

He was fond of him to the extent that he had lent him $30,000 on the very first day of their acquaintance. This money should enable the young man to make good his loss at the stock market. Bradley had proved to be worthy of the trust Adams had placed in him. He had shown Adams the shares he had bought with the money. Adams himself had also given him the tip about the Hanson Sons stock and it had turned out to be a very valuable one. Hanson Sons shares had gone up 21 points—a nice profit for Bradley.

'I have something for you!' said Bradley suddenly and made a face as if he was about to give a kid some candy.

Adams raised his eyebrows. 'So? Let's see!'

Bradley pulled a paper from his breastpocket. The paper was folded several times and looked like a newspaper. But it turned out to be a private stock report.

Adams read it carefully and the longer he studied

it the more excited he grew. 'I've never heard such rot!' he exclaimed. 'That man must be a fool!'

Bradley looked confused. 'I thought it would interest you,' he said, 'but to be quite frank I don't understand too much about it. Would you explain it to me, please?'

Adams nodded his head obligingly and began: 'Somebody—a Peruvian—it says here has found a gold mine with a very high yield. They estimate that the total yield will amount eventually to over 10 million tons of gold. These are official expert estimates. The Peruvian has purchased the land and now intends to found a joint stock company for the exploitation of his gold mine. His own contribution will consist of the land and the gold mine which will amount to about 30% of the original capital and he is seeking partners who can buy into the company for the rest of the stock.'

Adams' eyes, usually lacking expression, had begun to sparkle. He didn't care whether Bradley could follow his explanations or not. He rose from his chair behind the writing desk and made his exit through the door as fast as his limping gait would permit. Bradley waited in Adams' office. After more than an hour had passed he finally began to believe that he wouldn't see the old man again that day. He left the office.

Meanwhile, however, Adams developed an activity resembling an erupting volcano. He had gone to his actual office from where he issued orders to the banks of General Cosmic to put at his disposal the money needed for the purchase of the Peruvian stock. This amounted to roughly one and a half billion dollars and would bring a profit of nearly six billion according to his preliminary calculations.

Half an hour after Adams had read the prospectus he had a lengthy phone conversation with Señor Ramirez in Callao, the owner of the prospective gold mine. Ramirez was overjoyed to have found so quickly a partner for his enterprise and promised to send Adams the same day the expert appraisal by a reputable geologist.

That same evening General Cosmic Company made the largest single purchase ever known to have been transacted in the history of the financial world. Homer G. Adams bought $1,451,788,000.00 worth of shares of the newly-founded Peruvian Gold Company, representing altogether 71% of the total original stock.

This night the usually so level-headed Homer G. Adams was so excited that he could not fall asleep at all.

'Wait, wait!' yelled Raleigh. 'Don't shoot! We need him alive! He's only bluffing you with this weapon. Seize him!'

In vain Rhodan had been waiting for the moment when the four guards' attention would be sufficiently diverted for him to grab his thermo-ray gun. At least three of the men kept him every instant under surveillance.

Nevertheless, it was Raleigh's intervention at this moment which permitted Rhodan's escape from certain death.

It happened in a not very dramatic manner. In one of the two doors, which Raleigh's men apparently had left open, appeared the heavy-set figure of Captain Barina. He held a late model machinegun in his hands.

Rhodan was the first to spot him. A second later he was also discovered by the two guards standing off to the side behind Rhodan.

'Keep cool!' said Barina calmly. 'Any move and you're dead! Drop your guns!'

The men reluctantly released their grip on their pistols, which, noisily, one after the other, fell to the ground.

Rhodan put his psycho-raygun back into his pocket and brought out instead his pulseray weapon. '*That's* the thing I was telling you about earlier,' he remarked in an ironic tone.

Barina handcuffed the men while Rhodan kept him covered. None of the guards or Raleigh offered any resistance. Then they were placed in Rhodan's car.

Barina, who had come in his own car, closely followed behind Rhodan's car with his prisoners. Rhodan led the way up into the Sierra Nevada mountains. During the ride Rhodan sent a radio message to Terrania.

Around midnight the two vehicles arrived at a lonely area near Lake Tahoe. There a transporter jet of the New Power was already waiting for them. Rhodan handed over the prisoners and wrote instructions for Reginald Bell, requesting him to inform him immediately of the results they would obtain in

Terrania after interrogating Raleigh and his men.

At a quarter past midnight the powerful plane lifted off the shores of Lake Tahoe and disappeared in the nocturnal sky.

The next morning already the first news from the interrogation was presented.

Raleigh didn't remember anything. He no longer knew anything about the automated harrows and plough-shares he had been selling. Neither could he recall anything about the man he had planned to have killed by his four bodyguards.

He quickly proceeded to believe that he was being detained and questioned by some fools and energetically demanded his release.

Khrest, who was conducting the interviews, would not hear of anything of the sort. He knew that Raleigh had been under exceedingly strong hypnotic influence from the day he began selling his automated agricultural machines. This hypnotic spell had vanished as soon as it became evident that Raleigh's number was up.

For the time being Khrest had not yet been able to determine who the man was under whose hypnotic influence Raleigh had acted. He must either be a telepath of incredibly powerful ability or he must have used some mechanical hypnotic instrument.

Khrest was convinced that whatever Raleigh had done and experienced while he was under the stranger's influence, must still be buried in his memory somewhere. However, in those areas of his conscious mind which were no longer accessible to Raleigh's will. Raleigh was therefore not lying when he asserted he didn't have the slightest awareness of all those things he was blamed for.

Khrest was certain he could bring up to Raleigh's conscious awareness the contents of his subconscious memory banks, which in turn would provide valuable information for Rhodan. Unfortunately this would take several weeks to accomplish. This would not be of much help to Rhodan during his first phase of counter-attack.

Rhodan realized that he had come out safe and sound from this first encounter but still had lost the battle. Together with Barina he had made a thorough search of the facilities of the Farming Tool & Machinery the following night but had found nothing which might give him a clue as to the man or the power behind this enterprise.

On the contrary: he was now absolutely convinced that this whole episode with the robot-guided agricultural machines had been staged for the sole purpose of luring some important member of the New Power to Sacramento in order to capture him there. Raleigh had merely been the instrument to activate the mechanism of the trap. Undoubtedly he had known at once that his intended victim had arrived the moment Rhodan had phoned him under the assumed name of Wilder.

Rhodan had barely escaped from this trap with the vigorous support of Captain Barina.

But the unknown enemy had been warned and Rhodan had not succeeded in compensating for this disadvantage by obtaining further clues and new information from Raleigh.

For the time being there remained only the hope that Lieutenant Richman might have uncovered some news in Salt Lake City. Perhaps the trail could be pursued further from this point on.

The fact that no new incidents had occurred in Terrania during the past few days was hardly cause for relief. For this fact was most likely due not to the increased security measures around the important installations in the huge metropolis but perhaps rather to the fact that the unknown foe was preoccupied with other tasks in the meantime.

The day after the big purchase Elmer Bradley appeared again in Adams' office and paid back the money he had borrowed. Hanson & Sons had shot up amazingly all of a sudden—the second sensational event of Wall Street during this week—and Bradley had earned $15,000 above the $30,000 he had received as a loan from Adams.

Bradley paid back with stock. And he kept his earnings also in the form of shares. Adams tried to persuade him to keep the borrowed sum of $30,000. 'You've helped me to such a fabulous business coup,' he said smiling, 'that I'd like to show my appreciation in this manner.'

But he couldn't talk Bradley into accepting the money. He only indicated that he wanted to take a vacation with the financial gains of the past few days to recover his strength after the excitement of the whole transaction.

He said goodby to Homer G. Adams, who never laid eyes on him again.

For three days regular news came in from Lieutenant Richman. Its tone was not encouraging: *Nothing new so far! Am searching for clues!*

One consolation at least, Lieutenant Richman kept after the unknown opponent.

The fourth day no report came from Salt Lake City. Rhodan was worried but Captain Barina's optimistic outlook was increased by this lack of communication. 'No news in the case of Richman,' he explained, 'means he must have found something.'

Therefore they paid no special attention to Richman's silence.

But the same evening they read in the newspaper that the police in Salt Lake City had found a dead body in one of the storage sheds near the Union Pacific Railroad Station. The report also contained a photo and a description which left no doubt that the dead body was that of Lieutenant Richman.

That same night Rhodan and Barina drove to Salt Lake City. Barina had never been so silent as during these hours. It was quite obvious that he was blaming himself for not having paid sufficient attention to his colleague's safety.

In Salt Lake City they went to the police. Captain Barina revealed his identity while Perry Rhodan still pretended to be a certain Mr. Wilder, whose interest in Richman's murder remained a mystery to the police.

The clues they received were rather pitiful. Two

policemen on patrol duty had found the corpse. According to the coroner's report at this moment Richman seemed to have been dead for three hours at least. There were certain indications that Richman had been killed right on the spot where he had been found rather than his body having been brought there after he had been killed.

But the owner of the storage shed was a most reputable man who had a most reliable alibi that he could neither have been the murderer nor had any involvement in this case.

Barina and Rhodan spent the night in a hotel and when the next day dawned and the first papers appeared the world had ready a new sensation for them. This sensational news item did not concern Barina at all but Rhodan was all the more startled by it. So much so that he immediately interrupted his stay in Salt Lake City and flew to New York.

The newspapers were enormous headlines and sensational reports about one big news item:

GENERAL COSMIC CO. LOSES $1½ BILLION OVERNIGHT!

3/ A GLIMPSE OF THE ENEMY

The loss was far greater in reality.

General Cosmic was a concern consisting of a large number of apparently independent firms. What was generally known under the name of General Cosmic Co. was actually nothing but the administrative center of hundreds of subsidiary enterprises.

These facts had of course not remained unknown to the stockbrokers. Although Adams had organized his widely branched firm with utmost care, 20 out of 193 of the subsidiary companies only were known to be part of the GCC. Whoever was familiar with the proverbial curiosity of the stockbrokers was ready to admit that this alone represented a fabulous 'index of concealment.'

When the news spread that General Cosmic had suffered a loss of one and a half billion dollars a terrific slump took place in the stock market. Everyone tried to get rid of the stock they were holding in the 20 subsidiary firms. This in turn led the rest of the companies associated with General Cosmic, who were not known to belong to it, to sell their shares as fast as they could. This of course made matters even worse for the GCC. Fortunately, however, GCC owned at least 90% of the joint stock of all companies affiliated with it. As a result the loss was painful but not critical.

The sudden price drop was finally arrested when a number of sharp speculators began to buy up GCC stock that same afternoon. They believed this whole affair to be nothing but a successfully staged stock exchange swindle affording them a good opportunity to get rich quick. As it turned out later, they had calculated right. However not because the sudden crash had been caused by some tricky business but because the GCC was financially sound enough to weather such a storm.

Rhodan arrived in New York toward noon on the day of the castrophe. He went straight to Homer G. Adam's office where he found a man who had lost faith in himself and was close to a nervous breakdown.

Rhodan lost one precious hour trying to instill new courage in his desperate friend. His main argument was: 'The GCC disposes of a capital amounting to more than 200 billion dollars. Due to the debacle with the gold mine and the ensuing crash we've lost altogether four billions. This is less than 2% of our capital!

'It isn't worth your while getting so upset; there are more important things we have to do.'

It took quite awhile before Homer G. Adams was willing to listen to what these more important things were. Rhodan demanded that Adams tell him how this blunder had happened and what had led up to it. 'Not because I don't trust you,' Rhodan quickly added to his request, 'but mainly because some unknown powers have lately been at work quite obviously attempting to bring about our ruin. The New Power needs you, Adams; we hope to get on their track with your help!'

Homer G. Adams gave a thorough report. He always carried with him a micro-tape recorder. All his talks with Bradley or with other people had been automatically recorded this way. Rhodan was far more interested in these recordings than in Adams' own report.

Rhodan listened attentively to all the tapes, then played back for Adams the first conversation he had had with Bradley at the cafeteria near Wall Street.

Adams concentrated and listened.

'Do you notice something peculiar here?' asked Rhodan finally.

Adams thought awhile. Then he shook his head. 'No, nothing.'

'Would you say you are normally the type of man who lends money easily?' inquired Rhodan.

Adams protested. 'Never in my life. And for very valid reasons.'

Rhodan didn't insist on hearing these reasons. 'Then why did you lend $30,000 to Bradley?' he wanted to know.

Adams just shrugged his shoulders. 'Why? I liked the fellow right away. I've racked my brains many a time why I should feel such great sympathy for the young man ... but I simply was very fond of him.'

Rhodan pointed to the tiny recorder. 'Didn't you wonder why Bradley never wanted to know the reason you offered to lend him this sum?'

'No,' admitted Adams in surprise.

'Of course I have no information as to what psychologists would have to say there,' continued Rhodan, 'but the way I see it, you'd definitely expect if a young man were to be offered such a large loan from a total stranger that he would be inquiring the reason for such generosity.'

This made sense to Adams. He began to wonder why

he hadn't noticed this already earlier on his own.

'There's only one plausible explanation for this,' added Rhodan. 'The reason Bradley didn't ask you for your motives was simply because he knew for a fact how much you must like him. He was certain to begin with that you would offer him that money and fulfill any wish he would utter in your presence.'

Adams was dumbfounded. 'How could he have known that?'

Rhodan leaned closer to Adams. 'Bradley is in my opinion a most capable telepath. Besides he has undoubtedly the ability to give hypnotic commands with strong post-hypnotic effect.'

Rhodan's assumptions were soon to be fully confirmed. It turned out that there was no such person as Señor Ramirez in Callao with whom Adams believed he had had a phone conversation. And on top of that the ITT informed them that no phone call from the GCC's office had been made to Peru during the past three months.

Homer G. Adams had only imagined such a phone conversation had taken place. And this false memory had been the result of a post-hypnotic suggestion emanating from Bradley.

The prospectus for which Adams had fallen proved to be an obvious swindle which would have been detected normally by any mere beginner.

The final proof came following a psychological examination that Adams was requested to undergo. It was found that Adams' brain activity—even almost 48 hours after he had last seen Bradley—was abnormally slow, a sure sign he had been subjected to some recent hypnotic and suggestive influence.

There could no longer be any doubt that Adams had become the victim of that mysterious unknown person who had also been responsible for the thefts and explosions in Terrania, and who must also be behind Mr. Raleigh's robot guided agricultural machines.

This man was at this moment by no means as satisfied as one would have expected.

There was no doubt he had a number of successful actions to his credit now. But when he compared his actual achievements with his original expectations, he realized that only half of them had come true.

At present he was sitting in his command center, situated 99 feet underground. Together with a house built directly above it, it formed an unassailable fortress. The mystery man was conducting a conversation via TV with the young man whom Adams had known as Elmer Bradley.

The young man looked about as depressed as when Adams had first met him in that cafeteria near Wall Street in New York.

'What's the idea, you blundering idiot!' criticized Monterny. 'Your orders were to cause the GCC to incur a loss of at least 10 billion dollars. And what did you accomplish? A lousy four billion! What's the meaning of that?'

Bradley lived in a modest little house in just as modest a little town in Northern California. The TV channels used by Monterny, the mutant master, in order to communicate with his mutant slaves, were inaccessible to any surveillance.

Monterny's image didn't appear on the TV screen. The picture tube in Bradley's TV set produced nothing but a scrambled screen showing mainly a lot of white snow effects on a black background.

'I wasn't sure of myself,' answered Bradley, depressed. 'The data you supplied for me were so flimsy that anyone could see through them right away. I was sure my mission would be a total failure. How could a man like Adams possibly be deceived by that?'

'As you have been able to convince yourself,' remarked Monterny sarcastically, 'it happened even despite your silly doubts.'

Bradley looked very tired. 'Yes, you're right. But I was very glad when I finally could get away from there.'

Monterny's voice over the TV suddenly turned icy cold. 'You ruined my plan, Bradley! A coup which brought me within a hairbreadth of total success. You had enough time to thoroughly prepare this big blow against the GCC. Ten billion dollars was the lower limit I had set for this coup. With your talents you could have easily attained twice, three times that amount. If you can cause an enterprise of that size to lose over 10% of its capital, this usually spells the end of it.

'And all this depended on you, Bradley!

'You've let this opportunity slip through your fingers, Bradley! Out of fear you acted rashly, didn't prepare your job the way you should have! And what is the result? From now on I'll have to proceed extra cautiously in my attacks on the GCC, provided I can still even risk any!

'You'll have to undergo a new training session, Bradley!'

Bradley gave a start. When Monterny had first tracked him down, he had forced him, the outstanding telepath, to undergo an initial training session. Bradley was sure that even hell would be a picnic compared to that ordeal. The schooling served the sole purpose to activate Bradley's parapsychological talents to the utmost limit of his potential and to acquaint Bradley with the mutant master's goals. At the same time letting him come to the conclusion that there was no opposition possible against the master's dictates.

Bradley—who apart from his special talents had been a perfectly normal human being—had twice attempted to escape from Monterny's clutches.

And twice he had suffered the brutal force of the mutant master. Twice he had been subjected to that sudden mental hammer blow which wiped out his own will from one instant to the next, leaving only room exclusively for the master's orders. Orders which had to be carried out on the spot.

Bradley could well imagine that the second training session would not be any more pleasant than the first. But he did not object.

'Tomorrow somebody will come and call for you,' explained Monterny. 'You'll accompany him—and you will become a new man.'

Monterny ended the conversation. The confusion of bright lines on Bradley's TV screen faded and disappeared.

Then Monterny issued orders that further activities

of this group were to be transferred to his Japanese branch.

He promised himself greater chances of success for his future enterprises if they were carried out closer to the enemy's base.

Meanwhile in Terrania, Khrest the Arkonide had arrived at a stage during his psychological examinations of the prisoner Raleigh where he hoped to obtain the first important information.

Raleigh had spent the last few days in a trance and had no longer offered any resistance to Khrest's endeavors to penetrate into his subconscious mind.

Khrest realized how important the information eventually to be supplied by Raleigh might be for Rhodan. He asked Thora to assist him with the decisive examination.

Thora, the beautiful Arkonide woman, had been recovering from the shock she had suffered during her recent adventure on Venus.

Thora and Khrest were members of an Arkonide research cruiser which had been sent from the distant planet Arkon to explore this section of the galaxy which was over 30,000-light-years away. The cruiser which had been commanded by Thora crash-landed on the Earth's moon where it was discovered during Rhodan's first flight into space. At that time Khrest needed help. He was sick and nobody on board his spaceship could cure him. Rhodan procured medical assistance from Earth and realized at once the tremendous manifold possibilities which were put at his disposal with this Arkonide space vehicle that was the product of a far-advanced technology measured by terrestrial standards. Khrest supported Rhodan in any way he could, at first out of sheer gratitude for having saved his life, later out of inner conviction. Thora put up a constant opposition; she was only interested in returning to her home planet as fast as possible.

But her wishes were foiled—through some terrestrial powers who meanwhile had learned that the representatives of an alien race had landed on their moon. They destroyed the disabled cruiser with atom bombs. The only members of its crew to survive were Khrest and Thora, who had flown to Earth in a small spherical lifeboat with a diameter of 180 feet, when the attack took place.

This auxiliary vessel and the instruments it carried on board ensured Perry Rhodan absolute technical superiority for the newly-founded state—the New Power. Rhodan prevented a war which would have meant the end of earthly civilization. As a result he and his new state were recognized by the rest of the world powers. He successfully warded off the attacks from extraterrestrial intelligences that had been attracted to this part of the universe by the automatic emergency signal emitted by the stranded Arkonide cruiser. Rhodan brought about victory for an attacked alien race living in the Vega system 27-light-years distant from Earth. He captured an Arkonide super-spaceship from an alien race who in turn had seized this vessel as booty from a defeated foe. This super-spaceship became the nucleus of Rhodan's spacefleet. Then he set out on an odyssey lasting several years to find the planet of eternal life, an artificial planet guided by a race who lived in a spiritually collective existence and who caused their artificial planet home to orbit in a strange, unmathematical path around a number of fixed stars. Rhodan experienced the almost incredible phenomenon of cellular rejuvenation which gave him immortality—but there was one condition attached to this gift: he had to visit periodically every 62 years this artificial world, called Wanderer, and get a new treatment by the physiotron. Also Reginald Bell, Perry's friend, had received the gift of immortality.

The two Arkonides however had been refused this treatment. Their time had run out, their race was on the downgrade; only young, aspiring races were considered worthy to receive the gift of eternal life.

Nine years after Rhodan had discovered the Arkonide research cruiser on the moon, he returned to Earth. Conditions on Earth, that had been so stable when he had left on his search for the planet of eternal life, had in the meantime deteriorated. The Eastern Bloc was in revolt. A rival space landing division had become established on Venus in order to conquer there the base of the New Power which also harbored the mighty positronic brain.

Rhodan acted immediately. He attacked and dispersed the enemy's division, leaving enough people alive on Venus to give him hope that they might found a colony there far removed from any political ambitions—after they would have learned to adapt to the rigors of life in the Venusian jungle world. Having completed this task he returned to Earth and removed the obstacle for a final union of mankind which the opposition of the Eastern Bloc had represented.

And during all this time Thora had to resign herself to wait for the fulfillment of Rhodan's promise to permit her to return to Arkon as soon as the 'situation had become safe enough.'

Thora had thus waited for ten Earth years; then she took matters in her own hand: she fled to Venus in one of the newly built destroyers. She intended to activate the hypersender on the Venusian base and broadcast a signal for help toward her home planet Arkon. But she had overlooked the fact that the new ship had not yet been equipped with the special code sender which alone could permit access into the area surrounding the ancient Arkonide base on Venus. Her destroyer was therefore shot down and Thora was made prisoner by a group of survivors from the former space-landing division of the Eastern Bloc.

Rhodan, who hurriedly left Earth in pursuit of the fleeing Thora, shared a similar fate. He took off in the same type of destroyer ship and was of course also refused entry into the base and shot down by the positronic brain.

Rhodan was cut off from all assistance for the positronic, having been alarmed by the strange events, had placed a barrier around the entire planet Venus in order to prevent any further intrusions. Rhodan, almost single-handed, took up the fight for Thora's freedom. He won the battle, barely escaping with his life on several occasions.

He brought a much subdued, dejected Thora back to Earth, who had to promise him she would wait until he would accompany her on her return flight to her planet home.

To a certain extent, Thora was very pleased now that Khrest had requested her help. Without wanting to admit it to herself, she was eagerly waiting for a chance to prove to Perry Rhodan that she could be a quite useful person and not just an impatient haughty woman causing trouble and confusion. Perhaps examining the prisoner would offer such an opportunity to redeem herself.

Khrest was awaiting her. The room in which Raleigh was lying strapped on an examination table was rather large but at this moment so jammed full of instruments of all kind that there was hardly room in which to move around.

'What are you planning to do?' Thora asked in her own Arkonide language.

'Deep probe,' replied Khrest curtly.

Thora audibly drew a deep breath. 'Have you exhausted all other approaches?'

Khrest shook his head. 'I've tried everything. Assuming he still has a remnant of some memory of the incident with the unknown person who put him under his hypnotic spell, the memory is buried so deep that we can hope to reach it only with a special depth probe.'

Thora's face was serious when she spoke. 'Let's hope he'll survive this ordeal.'

Khrest rolled a little table with the complicated deep-prober instrument next to the examination table. 'Will you take charge of the electrodes while I watch the indicator?'

Without a word, Thora took the two spindle-shaped parts of the apparatus which were connected by two thick cables to the actual instrument, and fastened them to a frame above Raleigh's head. The thin ends of the spindles were now pointing at Raleigh's head.

'Ready?' asked Khrest.

Thora checked the position of the spindles. 'Yes, go ahead!'

A soft hum came now from the small apparatus. Thora kept watching the spindles. They remained undisturbed.

'Full charge!' said Khrest.

The prober-screen showed now the first wave reflexes—a confusion of green lines which for the time being could not be interpreted. Khrest made sure that the film camera attached to the apparatus was working. The film would later be presented to the positronicon for evaluation in order to decipher Raleigh's memories.

The tangle of lines on the screen showed up clearly. It became evident that Raleigh's brain was just an average specimen.

'Exchange the two spindles, please!' requested Khrest after some time had elapsed.

Thora made the change. A second period of radiation produced complementary pictures to the first ones they had already obtained.

The whole examination lasted about 15 minutes.

'That's it!' said Khrest. A switch clicked, a lever fell, the humming sound gradually died down. Nothing had changed all throughout the examination in Raleigh's facial expression. He was breathing quietly and regularly.

'He seems to have withstood it alright,' remarked Thora.

But Khrest was already busy with other things. 'Do you want to help me with the evaluation?' he asked.

Thora smiled. 'Are you feeling alright, Khrest? My diagnosis: A Terranian-type burst of activity! Here you are working as much in one hour as you would not have accomplished in one whole day back home on Arkon.'

Khrest returned the smile. 'Vitality is contagious,' he answered, 'or would you prefer lying under a cerebronicon and look at the wave patterns?'

Thora laughed out loud. 'No, no! I'd rather help you here!'

General Cosmic recovered. The prices of its stock began to rise and the speculators were eager and willing to buy.

But a few thousand miles toward the west a man tried very hard to secretly prepare the final death blow against General Cosmic and with it against the New Power. This time he wanted to make sure the job would be thoroughly planned and executed.

Clifford Monterny assembled his mutants in his Japanese branch and informed them of his intentions. 'This time we won't miss!' he declared. 'When we're through there won't be any more New Power nor Perry Rhodan left on the face of the Earth or anywhere else in the universe!'

Rhodan spent some time investigating the case of Homer G. Adams. He gratefully accepted the assistance of the Terranian Defense Federation, headed by Allan D. Mercant. He learned from Mercant's agents the location of the print shop which had produced the amateurish stock market prospectus describing the fictitious gold mine in Peru.

The shop was situated in a suburb of Osaka in Japan. Rhodan quickly found out further details. The owner of the print shop did not deny that somebody had come to him two weeks earlier and had placed an order with him to print this prospectus.

This was however as far as the trail led. Therefore Rhodan flew back to Terrania in the hope that Khrest would meanwhile have obtained some additional information from Raleigh.

The evaluation sector first had to dig through the maze of memories which had accumulated throughout a lifetime in Raleigh's brain. These memories had of course nothing to do with the Sacramento affair.

Images from his childhood, Raleigh's high school life, military service, years of studies at the Institute of Technology.

The E-sector rejected these images until it finally hit on the data they were looking for.

Khrest was startled when suddenly the first image of the series appeared which contained the desired information: the picture showed a man with hazy outlines and an unrecognizable face who somehow had materialized out of thin air right next to Raleigh's desk in his Sacramento office. Raleigh had been thoroughly frightened by this sudden apparition.

Thora stared unbelieving at the short sequence of pictures which Khrest projected over and over again in a loop. 'How can that be possible?' she gasped.

'Oh, yes,' replied Khrest, who himself could hardly overcome his surprise, 'from that instant on when this man suddenly appeared in Raleigh's office, Raleigh continued to be under his hypnotic spell. Apparently this influence could be temporarily increased or decreased according to need. For instance, Raleigh still remembers this incident but no longer the face or image of that man. The unknown made sure that Raleigh would never be able to identify him or that nobody else could do so rummaging around in Raleigh's memory banks. You see, Thora: no figure, no face, nothing but vague outlines!'

'That sounds,' remarked Thora, 'as if you don't believe that this hazy shape and the unknown foe are one and the same person; am I right, Khrest?'

Khrest nodded. 'You are right there, Thora. I am convinced that anybody who is so intent on never being recognized and identified by anyone, will never show himself during one of his actions. He sends his go-between—and even those are so disguised that the involuntary partner-in-crime won't be able to recall what they looked like. Not even the depth prober will bring this image to the surface.'

Khrest proceeded to project some more filmstrips: the first deliveries arriving by rail, the onset of the advertising campaign in the newspapers and TV, the first inquiries, the first orders, the first sales.

All these pictures were interspersed with scenes showing hazy-looking people, unidentifiable men, the hiring of the four guards.

And finally Rhodan's phone call. Raleigh's thoughts what he would do to him. Then Rhodan's visit, the

66

arrival of the bodyguards, Barina's intervention.

And finally—blackout! Nothing besides a few distorted scenes that already had taken place after he had been brought to Terrania. Then total darkness. The period during which Raleigh was resting on the examination table, the time he was in a deep trance.

Khrest sighed and switched off the projector. He stared at the shiny table top before him.

'Well,' began Thora, 'what have we found out now?'

Khrest did not hurry with his answer. When he spoke it was with deliberate slowness. 'We have learned that the unknown foe will almost never relax his hypnotic grip on his helpers and victims. They are kept under his unceasing surveillance via telepathy— sometimes stronger and sometimes weaker—but the influence is always present in some form.'

'What good will this information do us now?'

Khrest narrowed his eyes to mere slits. 'Telepathic influence can be detected by certain brains even if they are not the intended target against which it is directed. Hypnotic influence is also a five-dimensional sending-and-receiving process. There are some secondary areas due to dispersion, although a good telepath will usually work in a sharply delineated directional beam.

'As a consequence a similarly efficient telepath should be capable of perceiving the hypnotic beam if it is being received by one of the helpers and provided the two are not separated by too great a distance.'

These were the results of the examination which

were reported to Rhodan shortly after his arrival in Terrania. Raleigh and his men had been released; they no longer presented any danger for anybody.

At nearly the same time Rhodan received a radio call from Salt Lake City. Captain Barina informed him briefly that there had been no further developments in his efforts to track down Richman's murderer. Rhodan suggested Barina should give up the search. 'We have another lead here that might set us on his trail!' he explained and Barina felt very grateful to hear this new turn of events.

Rhodan felt, after all the data he had gathered and those he had received from Khrest's depth probe examination, that now the time had come to inform one of his mutants about the recent alarming incidents.

'I hope you will understand,' he finished his explanation to John Marshall, one of the members of Rhodan's mutant corps, 'we had no way of making sure at first if the unknown hadn't forced some of our own mutants into his service. Not until now did we find out that such was not the case. The enemy works only with his own people.

'But as long as we didn't know this for certain we didn't dare inform our mutant corps. Those of us who knew all along what was going on, were inaccessible to any sort of thought reading. If we had included one of you in our circle then his thoughts would not have remained a secret for very long to the rest of the telepaths among you—and our plans would have been revealed to our enemy.

'I hope you realize we didn't intend to slight you, it was just a necessary precaution.'

John Marshall, the Australian, looked at Rhodan across the table at which they were sitting. He smiled. 'I am convinced, sir,' he replied, 'that the other mutants will be just as delighted as I am that you finally see your way clear to include us in this affair.'

Rhodan hesitated awhile before he continued. 'You know that I have only very weak telepathic abilities and I can't read your thoughts against your will. But in this case you should nevertheless tell me what you really are thinking!'

Marshall's smile deepened. 'Alright, then, I'll give it to you straight: None of us will feel very flattered when they learn that you suspected the mutant corps at first. But once they learn the reasons for this then it ... it will be exactly the way I already have told you: we are happy to be included now in this affair and will do our best to cooperate with you.'

Then Rhodan proceeded to expound his plan of action to John Marshall. 'It will be so much easier for you telepaths than for the two teleporters,' Rhodan concluded. 'You are four people who can relieve one another by turns: you, Ishy Matsu, Betty, and Nomo Yatuhin. But Tako can alternate only with Ras Tschubai.

'Make sure to impress this on all the others: from now on both a teleporter and telepath will have to be on guard every single second. The telepath will have to locate the intruder while the teleporter will have to catch him as quickly as possible. We must not forget that anybody who is trying to intrude unnoticed in our territory is of necessity a teleporter. Therefore Tako and Ras must always carry weapons. But tell them that psycho-rayguns are totally ineffective.'

The most depressing part of this whole affair was that even John Marshall had no idea how the intruder would make his presence felt. He had never been confronted by a problem like this.

Marshall had taken up residence in a small apartment on the outskirts of the city. It was up on the 24th floor and the four telepaths used it as their guard headquarters.

They had arranged that each would be on guard duty for six hours a day. The two teleporters had to be ready for action 12 hours each and every day.

The one to take her task most seriously was little Betty Toufry. Betty was the strongest telepath working in the mutant corps of the New Power. At the same time she was just as powerful a telekineticist. Rhodan had discovered her when she was still a little girl. She had come along on the long trip to the planet Wanderer. Now she had reached the age of ten and with all the zeal typical for her age she mustered all her powers for the protection of the New Power.

This afternoon John Marshall came to relieve her from guard duty around six P.M. Betty looked quite dejected. 'Nothing happened. Again nothing at all.'

Marshall smiled at her. 'Don't worry, Betty. Something is bound to happen some day soon.'

'Will we really concentrate and watch out?' she asked eagerly.

'I promise I'll do my best.'

In the livingroom of the small apartment Tako Kakuta was lying on a couch reading a magazine. Marshall couldn't see his face but he heard him yawn.

'Good evening, Tako!' said John Marshall to the Japanese teleporter whose turn of guard duty was not up yet.

Kakuta put down his magazine. 'Good evening. Any news?'

Marshall waved his hand disparagingly. 'Nothing! What shall we do? Play chess, talk or read?'

Tako thought for awhile. 'Chess,' he said finally, 'if that's alright with you.'

'What's the difference how I kill the time?'

Kakuta sat up and pulled a little table closer to the couch. Marshall put his briefcase full of books on the floor—he had made sure he would have something along to while away the long tedious hours of uneventful waiting—and opened the door of the low cabinet where they kept their chess set.

It happened as he pulled out the set from the bottom shelf of the cabinet. He straightened up and hit his head against the edge of the top of the book cabinet.

Something strange, very delicate, seemed to reach into his brain. At first still hesitant, then it grew, became stronger and took the form of concrete orders —instructions directed toward some stranger who this moment had penetrated the domain of the New Power.

Marshall dropped the chess set. The noise startled the Japanese, who quickly jumped to his feet.

'He's here!' gasped Marshall. 'Administration building, between the 10th and 20th floor. Has orders to kidnap Khrest! Hurry up, Tako, get going!'

For the fraction of a second Tako stood rooted to the spot, his face bare of any expression, as if he hadn't understood what Marshall had told him. Then the air

71

was wavering and without any further warning the teleporter vanished. Marshall started to get busy now. He pulled a switch and established telecommunication with the administration building. Major Nyssen, acting as a substitute for the absent Reginald Bell, received the alarm signal. He took immediate care to have the entire wing of the building evacuated where the intruder had been reported to have penetrated. Major Nyssen took into consideration that the unknown hostile teleporter would need some time to find his bearings in the unfamiliar surroundings and that he would not be aware of the evacuation taking place. Tako Kakuta would need to be free from any interference to obtain best results.

Rhodan had been informed that the enemy apparently intended to kidnap Khrest. He was deeply worried, for Khrest was about the most precious asset the New Power could lose. The unknown intruder appeared to be very confident of attaining his goal. It was important to find out why he would feel so sure of himself.

Nyssen directed Marshall to leave his quarters at the outskirts of Terrania and to move inside the protective barrier dome. He was supposed to take up his new position in front of the main entrance of the administrative building, then to establish direct contact with Nyssen via micro-telecom. Thus he would be able to immediately inform the major, who was waiting in the command center, in case the intruder started making any unforeseen moves.

There was no change in the strange sensation that Marshall was subjected to as he was approaching the administration building. He was under the impression that this sensation was not related in any way to the distance that separated him from its source. He would have been hard put to describe this feeling. It was like a headache, a constant pressure, which quite unlike the usual type of headaches carried the information where it came from. Overlying the sensation of pressure he could clearly distinguish varying instructions directed toward the unknown teleporter.

Marshall established himself under the main portal of the gigantic administration building. He reported to Major Nyssen: 'Arrived at new location, sir. So far no new incidents to report. The man's moving very slowly; in any case he is not making any sudden displacements via teleportation.'

Tako Kauta's jump ended as planned in the main cross corridor of the 20th floor. The corridor was empty and brightly lit. Tako knew that in case of an alarm situation the endangered part of the building would be evacuated immediately.

Tako was wearing very light and soft shoes. He was marching along the passage without making any noise. Dead silence reigned all around him.

Tako didn't bother to enter and search any of the rooms leading off the corridor. He had heard from Marshall that the stranger was under orders to kidnap Khrest. Therefore he would not be staying in a room where at the first glance he could establish the fact that Khrest was not present.

Tako entered one of the gravitational elevators and went up to the 21st floor. Here too he limited himself to walking along the main corridor and then to checking the peripheral passages.

Nothing—no sound, no feeling of impending danger.

The same on the 22nd floor and the 23rd. Marshall had indicated the target area to be somewhere between the 20th and the 30th story. Tako had no idea exactly how Marshall could pinpoint the place. It was quite possible that he would have to go up as far as the 40th floor before he would find the stranger.

24th floor.

25th floor.

26th floor.

No call from the command center. The stranger still seemed to be moving along on foot.

27th ...

There it was!

Tako felt the peculiar drawing sensation for the first time in his life; but he knew at once that the enemy was right before him. He crouched in one of the recessed doorways and waited.

While he was waiting he tried to analyze the sensation he was feeling in his brain. What was it? Tako realized that he had no telepathic abilities at all. It was impossible that this gentle, constant pain should be caused by the stranger. But the intruder was subjected to a strong hypnotic influence. Perhaps this was what had warned the Japanese?

Tako heard a sound. He pressed himself even closer against the recessed door, then slowly advanced his head toward the edge of the niche so that he could look around it.

There stood the man!

Tako had a good side view of him. He was a young man. A Caucasian. He was studying the nameplates on the doors and didn't seem to know where he should go next.

He couldn't see Tako. Tako stealthily stepped out from his hiding place and pointed his thermoray gun at the young man before he spoke. 'Stay where you are! Put your hands above your head!'

Tako saw the stranger stiffen up with fright. The man's fingers spread apart as he slowly and hesitatingly raised his arms above his head. Cautiously Tako came closer. He was nearly 15 feet away from the stranger when he suddenly felt the overwhelming, powerful mental shock-wave emanating from the man's brain as he was readying himself for the teleportation jump that would save him.

This was what Tako had been counting on. The stranger would have been the first teleporter who would not have escaped from a threatening weapon by an immediate jump to safety.

Tako was in his own element! A fraction of a second was sufficient for him to grasp the wave pattern the man was radiating and with it the energy the stranger was activating for his leap. Five dimensional energies which are required for teleportation are vectors—a physical quantity with both magnitude and direction. The moment Tako had absorbed this pattern and adapted to it he knew not only the answer to 'how far?' but also to 'where to?'

He jumped the same instant the stranger did. Tako

was still holding his thermoray gun in his hand ready to shoot.

He was seized by the tugging pain of the teleportation. For one thousandth of a second all light seemed to be blotted out around him.

'He's jumped!' shouted Marshall excitedly. 'The stranger's gone, sir! He's disappeared!'

Nyssen reacted at once. Two seconds after Marshall had finished speaking the telecom line to Kakuta was established. 'Hey, Kakuta! Do you hear me?' called Nyssen. 'The guy has vanished. Return, please! All clear!'

There was no answer.

'Kakuta! Can you hear me?'

Still no reply.

Nyssen had a short conversation with Rhodan. He learned from him that teleporters have the ability to recognize the target of another teleporter who is executing a jump close by by absorbing the shock-wave pattern. It was therefore a foregone conclusion for Rhodan that Tako had followed the fleeing intruder.

Hardly an instant was left for Tako to look around the place to which his pursuit had taken him. He saw a moderately sized room whose walls, floors and ceiling were obviously made of reinforced concrete. There was a table, three old chairs and a locked wall cabinet. No windows at all. The room was illuminated by one lone neon tube, six feet long, fixed to the ceiling.

At the other end of the room, just a few yards away, the stranger had made his appearance out of thin air.

Tako was about to challenge him when suddenly an unknown power invaded his brain with unbelievable force.

Tako fell down headlong on the floor. The thermoray gun slipped out of his hand. Tako pressed his face against the cold floor and pushed both hands against his temples to fend off the horrible pain.

For nearly half a minute he was unable to move. With waves of alternating amplitude the alien influx was coursing through his brain, causing him to forget why he had come here and making a whimpering helpless bundle of human misery of him. But then he remembered that he had a special ability with which he could save himself. As fast as he could and as intensively as the pain would permit he concentrated on the place from which he had come. And the instant the strange influence relented for a brief moment and became bearable, he jumped. He felt how the piercing, flowing pain of teleporting was nothing compared to the agony he had endured in the last few seconds.

He was grateful to perceive the starry sky appear above him again. He felt the coarse-grained sand under his knees. He looked around.

He could see the lights of Terrania shining over to the west. He had landed some six miles from his intended destination.

The excessive exertion he had just gone through made itself felt. He tried to stand up but his legs gave way under him. He fell headlong and fainted. He came to rest on a tiny strip of yellow desert sand that had persisted despite all the artificial irrigation between two large garden plots.

4/ THE CLUE OF THE MICRO-FREUDS

'We have news from Kakuta!' reported Nyssen toward midnight. 'He's lying six miles east of the city between two gardens, too weak to move. He wants us to pick him up!'

Rhodan nodded his head in agreement. 'Get a car ready, Major!' he ordered Nyssen. 'I'll drive out there with John Marshall.'

Nyssen confirmed the order. Minutes later a car was waiting for them. Rhodan first picked up Marshall from his apartment in the city, where he and Ras Tschubai had again taken up guard duty against possible intruders. They drove toward the east perimeter of the city.

Rhodan was in communication with the Japanese via microtelecom. 'When you see our headlights, Tako,' he instructed the mutant, 'please direct us! We've no idea where you are. Is that clear?'

'Yes, sir,' replied Tako in a weak voice.

'How are you feeling?' inquired Rhodan.

'Just miserable,' came Tako's frank answer. A few seconds later he called excitedly: 'I can see your headlights, sir! You're on the right track. But keep a bit more to the north, please.'

Rhodan followed his request.

'Stop!' shouted the Japanese. 'That will do. Now drive straight to the east ... but please don't run over me.'

A few minutes and they finally found him. He was still lying flat on his back, hardly able to sit up on his own. Marshall and Rhodan lifted him up, put him in their car and then drove back to Terrania.

'How is he, Eric?' asked Rhodan.

Dr. Manoli shrugged his shoulders and looked quite dejected. 'Total exhaustion,' he answered. 'Never in all my life have I seen anybody so completely worn out as Tako Kakuta.'

'How long will it take till I can interrogate him?' inquired Rhodan.

'Oooh ... five to six weeks I would say.'

'*Weeks?*' Rhodan shouted in disgust. 'I don't think you realize how much depends on the evidence Tako can supply us. Use whatever you have in your medicine chest here and get Tako back on his feet in a couple of *hours*, you hear me?'

Dr. Manoli shrugged his shoulders once more. 'It's not only Tako's exhaustion we have to deal with,' he demurred. 'I've taken an encephalogram. His brain activity is quite upset and is only very slowly returning to normal. During his absence Tako must have been subjected to some extraordinary, strong mental influence ...'

Rhodan knitted his brow. 'Is it ... serious?'

Manoli shook his head. 'No, it's mainly confusion.'

'Hmm ... how long will it take you to put him back on his feet for at least two hours or so?'

Dr. Manoli pondered for a few seconds before he replied: 'Let's say ... about 10 hours.'

'O.K., that'll do. Let me know when he'll be ready.'

Tako Kakuta insisted on being out of bed, standing up and completely dressed when he would be seen by Rhodan. Dr. Manoli had suggested it would be preferable for his health if he were to stay in bed during the interview but Kakuta refused to do so.

'Then get up, you stubborn guy!' Manoli growled irritated, 'and don't forget to tell me in time if you're going to feel sick!'

Kakuta promised with a smile.

Rhodan received him in his office located on the top floor of the administration building. Tako sat down in a comfortable chair across from Rhodan. Then he began his report.

He didn't conceal anything—starting with Marshall trying to fetch the chess set from the cabinet, the sudden appearance of the unknown teleporter on the 27th floor of the administration high rise, till his total collapse in that unknown basement room with cement walls, and finally his return to Terrania.

Rhodan listened intently and didn't once interrupt Tako's account. When Tako had finished, Rhodan rose from his seat and walked over to one of the wide windows which afforded a marvelous view over the city and the surrounding countryside.

The window panes were almost free of reflections; the glass had been selected on purpose to provide as clear a view as possible. Only a very weak and vague picture of hazy outlines could be seen of Tako Kakuta, who was now sitting diagonally behind Perry Rhodan.

'I suppose you've never seen that strange teleporter

before, Tako?' asked Rhodan. He was satisfied to observe a blurred image on the window pane as Tako shook his head behind him, still sitting in his chair.

'No,' said Tako, 'he was a complete stranger.'

'I wonder,' continued Rhodan, 'did you see him clear enough that you would have recognized him without any doubt if you had ever met him previously?'

A hazy movement in the almost completely transparent glass. It was Tako as he nodded and answered: 'No doubt about it.'

Another movement, this time a bit lower, near Tako's hip.

'Do you have any idea what the location of the place is where you landed after your tele-jump?' Rhodan inquired.

The answer came promptly. 'I could jump right back to the same spot if that's what you mean, sir. But I don't think I'd be able to give the geographic coordinates.'

Tako was performing all kinds of hasty movements while he was talking. Nevertheless, Rhodan let him go on speaking until he had finished. Even then Rhodan let several seconds pass before he said in a harsh voice: 'You're holding a neutron raygun in your hand, Tako! Who the devil gave you that? In the last few seconds we've been talking, you've been busy getting the weapon ready to use. And now you want to kill me. It won't work!'

Rhodan whirled around and stared at the Japanese mutant. Tako's face, normally so friendly, harmless and gentle had changed to a fierce grimace full of hatred and thirst for blood. Tako had raised his right hand and pointed the neutron raygun directly at Rhodan. Tako's hand was absolutely steady.

Rhodan smiled although it cost him quite an effort.

Tako's right index finger curled tightly around the broad trigger. A weakly fluorescent ray, hardly the breadth of two fingers, shot out from the barrel of the weapon.

The same moment, a layer of air about five feet in front of Rhodan, reaching from the floor to the ceiling, lit up, creating an artificial wall of painful brightness. The protective barrier screen absorbed the tremendous energy of the neutron ray amidst noisy crackling, then activated the energy reserves of the raygun and de-voured these too.

Rhodan heard Tako scream aloud in pain—then silence. The crackling of the protective wall died down the same instant. Rhodan waited until the light effect vanished. Then he went to care for Tako.

Tako had slipped from his armchair and was lying on the ground. His hand which had held the weapon showed two fresh burns. The excessive strain placed on the weapon had caused an electric charge to flow from the high potential of the neutron generator over to Tako's hand. The electric shock had rendered Tako unconscious.

Rhodan informed Dr. Manoli of the outcome of the interview with Tako, then called an ambulance to take the Japanese away.

'A hypnotic block of tremendous intensity,' explained Perry Rhodan, 'so skilfully applied that

Manoli's rather superficial examination of Tako's brain activity could not detect any trace of it.'

Khrest was staring pensively at some invisible point in the air. 'What kind of a monster would be capable of this?' he murmured.

'If we assume that the unknown does not master the Arkonide psychophysics and consequently does not possess any mechanical instruments that would enable him to influence other people in such a powerful manner—then he must indeed be a monster.

'Can Manoli handle this situation?' wondered Khrest, suddenly very concerned about Tako's safety.

'Don't worry about Manoli's skill!' Rhodan replied. 'He knows his business—and also all the new tricks he needs. But it looks like we may have to let Tako take it very easy during the coming weeks.'

'Does he remember anything about the whole affair?'

'Oh, yes! He knows everything—from the moment when he cornered the stranger till the second when he landed in Terrania again. But if anyone tries to tell him that he made an attempt on my life he tells them they're crazy. The moment he got rid of the hypno-block also meant the end of any memory of what his hypnotic orders had been.'

All were quiet for awhile, each lost in his own thoughts. Then Khrest broke the silence: 'What next? What are your plans, if any?'

'Right now my plans still seem to be very difficult to put into action ... but I do have some.'

Khrest's reddish eyes showed interest. 'We must

learn to interpret and transpose Tako's tele-jump patterns into exploitable geographic data.'

Khrest sucked in his breath noisily. 'To interpret and transpose! That's a big order! Do you have any idea whether such a thing is even possible?'

Rhodan laughed. 'No, not the faintest.' He rose from his chair. 'I'll make it my foremost duty to find out if there is any chance of success for us in this matter. If not then we'll have to try some other approach.'

Rhodan walked over to the door and as he was about to leave the room he turned around and said to Khrest: 'There is one thing I am particularly happy about: the whole story about planning to kidnap you was nothing but a big bluff. Maybe the intruder actually felt a command to seize you. But in reality he came here merely to lure one of us to follow him to his home grounds.'

Khrest wrinkled his forehead. 'Do you really believe that I wasn't the one they were after?'

'I'm positive!' laughed Rhodan. 'After all it would be sheer megalomania for anyone even to think about trying to abduct you right from the very center of the New Power's domain.'

Clifford Monterny had experienced his first major defeat in, so to speak, a direct line of transmission.

He had maintained a one-sided, unnoticeable tele-pathic contact with the Japanese Tako Kukuta until Tako's hypno-block had been removed by a psycho-physical method. And before he could manage to re-establish the interrupted connection, Tako had been given a counterblock which even the mutant master himself was unable to pierce.

The fact that gave Monterny the greatest cause for alarm was his inability to figure out how Rhodan had been able to outguess him. How could Rhodan have gotten any wind of the planned assassination attempt? Tako Kakuta had not given himself away with any word or gesture. During the medical checkup after his return, Dr. Manoli's first concern had been Tako's physical well-being. The mental tests had been so superficial and routine that even a far less skillfully placed hypno-block would have remained undetected.

Nevertheless ... !

Monterny assumed that Rhodan was not mutant—that is, he suspected this with almost complete certainty. Rhodan did not possess any clairvoyant, telepathic or any other talents with which he could have seen through the Japanese.

Still he had known in advance what was going to happen. At exactly the right moment he hid behind a protective screen and had thus caused the intended assassin's shot to riccochet from the energy barrier while he watched with calm assurance. The pain Tako had experienced when he was hit by the electric shock had been so violent that even Monterny had felt it.

Since Monterny was convinced that Rhodan was not a mutant, Monterny had to assume that Rhodan's behavior in face of an impending attempt on his life was the result of almost superhuman circumspection and an outstanding talent for combining the merest hints into workable hypotheses. This notion enraged

Monterny to such an extent that he was incapable of forming a clear thought for several hours.

For apart from his tremendous thirst for power, Monterny also was convinced that he as a mutant represented a human being of a higher order. There was nothing worse for him than being found out by a mere 'normal' person.

The following morning Monterny had a longer discusion with McMurray, his closest associate.

Of all the mutants in Monterny's service, McMurray was the only one ever to have seen him face to face. The first time it had happened in Sacramento and from then on they met again and again.

McMurray was so firmly in the grip of Monterny's hypnotic influence that he had long since lost his own individual personality. However accompanying this loss of his true identity was a parallel increase of his parapsychic abilities. Tele-jumps across interplanetary distances had become in the meantime no longer anything unusual for the young man. During his leaps he could generate around himself such powerful and extensive transition fields that he could carry along large objects easily.

Just because of this talent McMurray generally played a most important role in Monterny's plans.

'It's going to be difficult but not impossible,' was Rhodan's reply to Khrest.

A series of diagrams with Tako Kakuta's pattern of teleportation jumps, recorded by a psychoanalyzer, were on the table before them.

'What have you been able to ascertain so far?' asked

Thora. 'The approximate target within a radius of about 60 miles.'

'And where is that?'

Rhodan picked up the diagrams and a map was revealed underneath. It was a map of the Japanese islands. 'Here!' said Rhodan, pointing to a circle outlined in red. 'Somewhere inside this circle.'

Thora regarded the map. A bit sarcastic she finally said, 'That's a tall order! Within this circle are located three major cities along with 12 million inhabitants: Kobe, Osaka and Kyoto. To this you must add another five million people living in the surrounding countryside—When do you propose to get through with your search?'

'I'm not looking for any of these 17 million inhabitants of this area,' countered Rhodan with a smile, 'but a basement built of reinforced concrete ... in case you've forgotten, there are not more than a thousand cellars of this type in all of Japan!' He put the diagrams back on the table. 'Besides, I hope to obtain still further data from Tako's tele-jump patterns. And finally I have noticed something else!

'Do you remember Homer G. Adams' suicidal maneuver at the stock market? He was fooled by an amateurishly written prospectus about some Peruvian gold mines. We succeeded in finding out where this prospectus was printed.'

'Yes, and where was that?'

'In a Printshop in Osaka!'

The man whom Rhodan sent to Osaka was Major Nyssen.

Nyssen did not leave unprepared. He was given a report about all the events leading up to his current assignment and was asked to study it thoroughly for a day. In addition to that he underwent a rapid training course in the Japanese language through the Arkonide hypno-training instruments.

Lastly he received a device, developed and perfected the previous day, which would protect him against any hypnotic influence. When he was shown the new device he started to laugh. The instrument was nothing but a glittering metal helmet which fitted over the entire skull and was capable of producing an anti-hypnotic field with the help of a tiny generator. 'Am I supposed to run around with that contraption on my head?' He wanted to know.

Rhodan nodded. 'Yes, from the very moment that you have the impression that the unknown enemy has become aware of your presence. I'd strongly suggest you wear this helmet. You know only too well what happens to unprotected persons.'

Nyssen took the helmet.

Major Nyssen had joined Rhodan's forces when he was rummaging through the wreck of the Arkonide research cruiser which originally had crashlanded on the Moon and had subsequently been destroyed by atomic missiles of the Western Bloc. As a matter of fact Nyssen had been on this bombing mission just a few weeks earlier. As far as looks were concerned he could have been Reginald Bell's brother: short, not quite as hefty, the same crewcut, although his hair was thinning and dark blond rather than the shade of carrots. His voice always sounded as if he had just woken up from a terrific hangover.

Nyssen flew to Shanghai with the daily clipper. He stayed one day in Shanghai trying to shake anyone trying to shadow him. That same evening he flew on to Tokyo. He repeated his maneuvers to get rid of any possible people on his trail and that same night took the Tokyo-Kobe express in order to get to Osaka.

It was 1:30 in the morning when he reached his destination. He had changed his outer appearance a bit. Usually a very dapper man, he was now wearing a rather shabby suit, although it looked as if it had seen better days and had originally been made by an excellent tailor. His shirt was faded and had an outmoded collar. He chose a hotel which seemed to fit his own impoverished appearance.

The disguise was very simple but effective. Anyone seeing him thought him to be one of those globe-trotters who came to the Far East with the sparse remnants of their fortune because either the police of their home country were after them or because they hoped perhaps to make an easy fortune here.

Nyssen rented a room on the 30th floor of a shabby hotel high rise. He devoted the first day to recovering from the strain of the past days. He spent many hours in a deep, dreamless sleep.

'You know your job!' Monterny said in a friendly tone. 'Just bear in mind that a great deal depends on how you complete this task.'

McMurray, who lately had been made the mutant master's confidante, promised: 'I'll certainly remember that.'

'And don't make the same mistakes as that fool Bradley! Allow yourself sufficient time! As far as I can see you won't run any risk this way.'

McMurray nodded obediently.

'I'm expecting your reports right on the dot at the agreed time!' Monterny reminded him.

McMurray nodded once more like an obedient automaton.

Then he left.

He went to his room—if one could indeed call the place a room: it had no windows, it was illuminated by a single neon tube along part of the ceiling, its walls were made of reinforced concrete. McMurray quickly packed the few belongings he would need for this enterprise. Above all his automatic pistol, the only weapon a teleporter could rely on when he suddenly made his appearance inside some strange territory after a tele-jump.

The vessel filled a medium-size suitcase. McMurray held the suitcase under his arm and stood in the middle of his room as if he were just trying to remember whether he had forgotten something he still needed to take along.

A few seconds later, however, the outlines of his figure began to grow blurred and shortly afterwards he vanished completely.

McMurray was on his way to execute the most serious blow that his master had ever planned against the New Power.

Nyssen had a pretty good idea what he could allow himself to do in Osaka and get away with it.

Included in those things that carried too great a risk was, for instance, a visit to the printer's shop where the stock market prospectus had been printed. Rhodan himself had paid a visit a few days earlier to that shop. And if that printshop was connected in any way with the mysterious unknown enemy, which probably was the case, then Rhodan's visit had been carefully registered, even if he had not been recognized.

Nyssen wanted to make sure to remain incognito as long as possible and acted accordingly. There was nothing easier in a city the size of Osaka than to find some people who would be willing to pull the chestnuts out of the fire for anyone ready to pay the right price.

Nyssen scouted around for such a person. Osaka was a harbor city. He spent a whole morning strolling through the harbor area and he was not disappointed in his expectations.

More than a dozen men accosted him and started a conversation which left no doubt in his mind that they were exactly what he was looking for. Nyssen noticed with satisfaction that evidently it must be written all over his face what he wanted to find.

He was very choosy. Toward 10 o'clock he almost hired a young fellow who looked so desperate that one could not fail to wonder how he happened to have landed in such a neighborhood. But in the end, Nyssen let him go after all. The risk was too great that the young man would some day get moral scruples and then run to the police to unburden his guilty conscience. Finally at 11 : 30 he decided on a short fellow with cunning eyes who sidled up to him and declared in broken English: 'Me ... Michikai. Michikai do everything ... You pay well ... Michikai your man!'

Nyssen grinned. Michikai appeared to be about 40-years-old and was a good half a head shorter than Nyssen. 'Me ... Jeremy ... Jeremy pays well ... You do everything!'

He spoke these words in Japanese and tried to imitate Michikai's broken English. Michikai made a startled face. Then he laughed and when Nyssen joined him with a good-humored chuckle, that clinched the deal.

They went together to a little restaurant where they took care of the details. Of course, Nyssen did not explain to his new collaborator what this deal was actually all about. He just hinted that he would like to get some information about the setup of this print-shop and this job seemed so easy to Michikai that he was quite amazed when Nyssen gave him an advance of $30, promising him the same sum again if he got satisfactory results.

Nyssen arranged with Michikai that from now on they would communicate with each other only by phone. This meant that Michikai would be at a certain restaurant at certain set hours where and when Nyssen would be able to reach him.

Michikai, on the other hand, could not get in touch with Nyssen, neither by phone nor directly. Nyssen wanted to make sure the unknown foe would not be able to trace him through his middleman.

Ted McMurray looked at the city with amazement. He had never laid eyes on it before. It appeared to him more beautiful than anything he had ever seen.

He had made his instantaneous appearance on the northern shore of the Salt Lake. The glittering surface of the lake lay between him and Terrania.

McMurray was lost in his admiration of the wonderful sight before him until he 'heard' from Monterny. Although the command was beamed with moderate energy, McMurray understood it very clearly. 'I said you needn't rush! But this doesn't mean you stand around gawking! Get to work!'

McMurray started to move. He knew what had bothered Monterny. It was not so much the fact that he had taken a good long look at the city. It was expected from an agent that he would thoroughly examine his future field of action.

Monterny knew the thoughts of his people. He had sensed the admiration which McMurray had briefly felt for that city. And this was the cause for his irritation.

McMurray made his way through the uninhabited green-belt which separated the city from the surrounding desert. After awhile he was able to distinguish details on the houses of the northern suburbs of Terrania. Then he teleported into the city.

Monterny followed his progress attentively. He realized that this mission represented a certain personal risk for himself. Monterny had found very quickly how the first teleporter he had dispatched to Terrania had been spotted and then pursued by Tako Kakuta. He knew that Rhodan counted some powerful telepaths among the members of his mutant corps. Therefore Monterny might endanger not only Mc-

Murray but also this entire mission if he kept in constant touch with the young man.

He kept him under observation by absorbing McMurray's radiations but he himself wanted to act as a sender only in extreme emergency.

The matter was too important.

Nyssen phoned the restaurant and asked to speak to Michikai. Michikai answered by identifying himself with his real name whereupon Nyssen inquired: 'Have the peach trees started blooming already in the southern part of Kiushu?'

Michikai cleared his throat and replied: 'Not yet. But it's almost over in Hondo.'

'Fine,' answered Nyssen. 'What's new?'

'I've looked the printshop over.'

'Discretely and inconspicuously as we agreed, I hope.'

'Absolutely. I pretended I wanted to place a large order but couldn't come to terms with the owner. We haggled over the price. So I left. But in the meantime I had seen everything, except for ...'

'Except for what?'

'There was one room which I couldn't enter. But I'd bet that it isn't any bigger than 50 square feet. It had only one door and I managed to catch a glimpse through it for a moment.'

'Didn't you at least try to get inside?' asked Nyssen.

'Oh, yes. When I left I pretended to mistake that door for the exit. The owner of the shop didn't like this a bit. He became quite angry and caught me just as I had opened that door for a split second. He slammed the door and maneuvered me to the real exit.'

'Hm,' grumbled Nyssen. 'Did you see what was in that room?'

'Yes. A videophone.'

'Anything else?'

'No.'

'Listen, Michikai: go to the post office in the central railway station. You know where the private lockers are. Go to the man at that window and say the password "Hokaido" number 7415. He'll then open that box for you. You'll find your $50 inside. I'll phone you again in a few days.'

'What, only $50!' squeaked Michikai, although he had only been promised another 30. But he was used to pretending to be outraged; sometimes it worked.

But before he could add another word, he heard a click in the phone. Nyssen had put down the receiver on the hook.

Nyssen had more important things to do now than to listen to Michikai. He was busy figuring out which time of the day would be most favorable for the new coup he was planning.

He had used his time well to gather information what a typical day in the life of this city was like. There were peaks and lows in its activity but never a completely quiet time.

Nyssen chose the hours between one and four in the morning. Three hours should be sufficient, he thought, to make a thorough search of the little print-shop.

He spent the rest of the afternoon sleeping, had a

good dinner, then went to a show which let out shortly before midnight.

He returned to his hotel, armed himself with those items he considered indispensible and useful for his enterprise. He picked about 20 different instruments; but thanks to the superior skill of the Ferroniam micro-technicians they didn't take up much space: he could easily accommodate all in two of his trouser pockets and in the breast pocket of his suit.

The heavy neutron raygun he carried, however, in a shoulder holster.

Shortly before one A.M. he arrived in the vicinity of the printshop. He was pleased to note that the street was almost deserted. If he could manage to open the entrance door to the building within three minutes, he would then be safe.

He needed $3\frac{1}{2}$ minutes; but nobody came to disturb him. He was confident that no one had seen him.

The entrance with the reception desk and the adjoining rooms with the printing presses Nyssen knew through Rhodan's and Michikai's descriptions. He didn't bother to search those. Without any further difficulties he entered the largest and best-furnished office and looked there for the door about which Michikai had spoken to him.

There were five doors altogether in the office. The one Nyssen was interested in was the only one the owner had taken the trouble to lock.

The lock was simple. It didn't offer any resistance to Nyssen's micro-tools for more than 20 seconds.

The small room behind the door had no windows. Nyssen closed the door behind him, switched on his tiny but very bright high-intensity lamp and looked around for a place where he could put it down.

Besides the v'phone Michikai had mentioned there was only a chair. Nyssen placed the lamp on the chair and wondered where he should now start his search.

He felt somewhat foolish as he began to knock on the walls. Some spots sounded hollow but on closer inspection with his miniature X-ray rod he noted that this was merely due to some mortar being knocked loose from between the bricks.

He spent one hour like this and slowly arrived at the conviction that he wasn't going to find anything at all here.

Suddenly he heard a deep humming sound coming from behind. He whirled around and saw the video-phone screen light up gradually.

He turned away from his wall and regarded the screen. It was most unusual that a v'phone would start off on its own. The picture screen wouldn't light up till the connection really had been established. This could definitely not be the case here for nobody had lifted the receiver. Nyssen hadn't heard any buzzing or ringing to announce a call.

He positioned himself in such a way that he was out of the line of vision of the picture phone's camera-picture sender. Then he waited.

He heard the click in the receiver the same moment he hastily switched off the lamp.

The receiver had not been lifted and still the video-phone came to life!

Nyssen slid along the wall a bit closer to the instrument and listened to the metallic voice which just had begun to speak. This phone must have a specially powerful amplifier for Nyssen was able to understand every word without even having the receiver close to his ear.

'... important meeting tomorrow evening at 8 o'clock ... at my house. Everybody is to come to the meeting ...'

Nyssen's attention was partially diverted by the peculiar image that appeared on the reception screen. It was a maze of jumbled lines. At first sight it looked as if something had gone wrong with the reception but then Nyssen became aware of a certain regularity with which the jerking, whirling lines were flitting across the screen.

He took his little camera from his pocket and snapped some pictures of the lines on the screen. But he had hardly started when the lines faded away. The reception had come to an end. Still Nyssen hoped that the experts would be able to obtain some results from a reading of this apparent confusion.

He had been able to listen only halfway and had gathered that the announcement contained no important clue for him. The metallic voice had spoken only of things which must be familiar to the members of this mysterious organization. There was no hint where the mentioned items were located or what they were. He gathered that the members needed no allusions in order to understand what it was all about.

Nyssen placed all his hope now in the few pictures he had been able to shoot.

It was getting late. Nyssen didn't resume his sytematic examination of the walls for hollow spaces. He was almost certain there was nothing to find behind these walls.

Instead he now concentrated his attention on the amazing videophone which began to work without having been switched on and whose receiver transmitted sounds while it was still resting on the hook.

There was an ordinary-looking but rather thinnish cord leading from the set to the wall. The cord disappeared into the wall a few inches below the videoscreen. Nyssen inspected the cord closer and found that it passed through the wall horizontally.

He decided therefore to leave the windowless room and returned to the larger office to look for a way that he could get to the other side of the wall. A door opened onto a little courtyard in the back of the building. One of the courtyard's walls seemed to be what Nyssen was looking for.

It didn't take him long: he found where the thin cord emerged from the wall, then ran up to the roof.

And on the roof he saw a large antenna!

Nyssen whistled softly through his teeth. V'phone sets, just like regular phones, were attached to some network. They received the speech and image impulses through wires and lines which ran underground inside the city and were strung between wooden or plastic telephone poles across the countryside. A telephone therefore didn't need an antenna and neither did a videophone!

This then was not a normal v'phone! It was a sender and receiving installation which worked without the intermediary of wires. It merely had been disguised as a videophone in order to fool any visitors.

And that explained why it had started to work without anyone having lifted the receiver off the hook!

Nyssen was in a rather pensive mood and decided to terminate this nocturnal visit. He was still pondering the matter when he unlocked the door to his room back in his hotel.

As was his habit he first unpacked the various measuring instruments and placed them carefully on the table, one beside the other.

Then he read the various gauges and scales, still absorbed in thoughts about his puzzling findings and quite convinced that the instruments would not show any readings.

Radioactivity—none!

Temperature—what nonsense? He would have noticed it right away if he had run into a heatwave—normal!

Telepathic-hypnotic interference ...

The instruments were so tiny that Nyssen had to use a magnifying glass in order to read the scales. Muttering a curse under his breath he removed the magnifying lens from his left eye and placed it in his right.

But the reading remained the same.

Telepathic-hypnotic interference—the indicator had moved over to plus six on the scale!

Nyssen removed the lens from his right eye and started ahead.

The measuring instrument was telling him that he had been exposed to some hypnotic influence. Plus six on the scale corresponded to six micro-freuds—that was sufficient to hypnotize a dozen adult men.

But he hadn't noticed anything at all! Or? Was he still subjected to that hypnotic force?

Well, thought Nyssen, it would be easy to find some explanation why I failed to be aware of it. Each brain has its own particular range of frequencies. Somebody might have been sending on a frequency to which my brain won't react. The frequency is measured integrally by the instrument. It will measure everything of a hypnotic nature that is broadcast within its range.

But where the devil did this hypnotic interference originate?

The moment the only possible explanation occurred to Nyssen, he was ready to pack up his instruments again and pay a second visit to the printshop. But he abandoned the idea after checking his watch. Four-thirty A.M.—too late!

Of course! The wave pattern on the videoscreen! Nothing had been wrong with the set. There had been no bad reception and neither had this been a product of some alien, geometrical fantasy—this then was the source of the hypnotic influence his instrument had registered!

5/ KHREST—KIDNAPPED!

In view of McMurray's phenomenal mobility it wasn't difficult at all for him to locate his victim after only a few hours.

McMurray fixed in his memory the face and figure of that man and then proceeded to study his habits, his daily comings and goings.

For Ted McMurray intended to abduct that man. By teletransportation. As a teleporter who had not been schooled by an Arkonide activation of the brain it represented a considerable difference whether he executed the tele-jump alone or whether he had to carry along with him some object similar to himself in size. A solo tele-jump involved for him a brief act of spontaneous release of energy but for a double-jump he needed a period of at least 10 minutes utmost and undisturbed concentration.

McMurray therefore tried to find some time during the fortunately rather monotonous life pattern of his victim which could accommodate this 10 minute interval with the minimum risk to himself. Those hours when this man was most likely to be alone.

It took two days for McMurray to orient himself.

He set the time for between 20:00 and 21:00 o'clock local.

Rhodan was convinced that no further information

could be obtained from the tele-jump pattern which Dr. Manoli had extracted from Tako Kakuta's brain.

The target area which he had encircled on the map had shrunk to roughly 28 square miles.

The circle only slightly touched the city of Osaka. There was a great probability that their goal was located outside the confines of the city.

This made the search easier. A house with a reinforced concrete cellar had to be quite large by Japanese standards.

As soon as Rhodan had gathered all the results he called Khrest.

But Khrest did not answer.

Rhodan got in touch with Thora.

Thora hadn't see Khrest for at least three hours.

Rhodan waited another five minutes and then tried again to reach Khrest.

But this time he had no better luck than before.

Then Rhodan remembered the order the foreign teleporter had been given when he had invaded the administration building in Terrania and which had been foiled when Tako Kakuta had met and then followed him to the fateful trap.

Rhodan sent out a general search alert for Khrest.

One hour later there was no longer any doubt that Khrest was nowhere to be found within the area of the New Power.

And he hadn't left any message where he had gone to or stated any other reason for his absence.

Khrest had been kidnapped!

By extrapolating backward they arrived at the most

probable time the kidnapping might have occurred: during the half hour between 20:00 o'clock and 20:30. For a short while later Rhodan had for the first time tried to get in touch with Khrest.

During these minutes Ishy Matsu, the slender Japanese mutant girl, had done her stretch of guard duty. She stated she had received a relatively strong but undecipherable single impulse at about shortly after 8 P.M. Since this impulse hadn't reoccurred she had paid no further attention to it.

Rhodan informed Thora that someone had abducted Khrest. He had never seen the proud Arkonide woman as upset as on this occasion.

'What ... what are you going to do about it?' she asked.

Rhodan stared at her in amazement. 'Attack! What else?'

'But where? Haven't you ...'

'Oh, yes I do. I have all the data I need. Perhaps Nyssen has detected meanwhile some additional information that will be useful to me. We're leaving at once.'

'By matter transmitter?'

Matter transmitters were one of those marvels that Rhodan had brought back from his expedition when he had gone in search of the planet Wanderer. These mechanisms would replace the parapsychic gift of teleportation for any person traveling inside their cage by transporting them via the fifth dimension to any place where a correspondingly adjusted receiving set was stationed.

Rhodan shook his head. 'No, not from here, if that's

what you mean,' he answered Thora's question. 'We don't have enough information about the circumstances at the other end of the line. Within the next five hours a special detachment will fly to Osaka. They'll be taking along some transmats and will be able to use them once the area has been properly reconnoitered!'

The hour between six and seven in the morning was one of the periods when Michikai was supposed to wait in the little restaurant for Nyssen's call.

Nyssen had slept for two hours and phoned shortly after six o'clock. He was told that Michikai wasn't there.

Nyssen repeated his call half an hour later but Michikai still hadn't shown up. Nyssen assumed that this little Japanese spy must have picked up his reward of $50 and split. He wasn't disturbed by this on general principles but still right now it was a nuisance when he could have made use of Michikai's services.

Contrary to his decision to remain incognito throughout this mission he drove to the restaurant where Michikai should have been waiting for his phone call. Maybe the owner of the little eating joint could give him some hint where Michikai might be found.

Everything had happened so fast for Khrest that he still hadn't quite comprehended what had taken place. A young man had suddenly appeared beside him while he was in his bedroom and had knocked him out. When Khrest came to he was lying in a room which strongly resembled the one Tako Kakuta had described having landed in when he had tele-jumped after the strange intruder.

Khrest felt only a very mild headache, which led him to believe he had been hit over the head not too violently and that he had remained unconscious for not too long a time. But according to Tako's statements this room was supposed to be situated in Japan —some 2500 miles from Terrania.

How could he have gotten here so fast?

Could there be any other installations of this kind, perhaps in the immediate vicinity of Terrania?

Not until some time later did it occur to Khrest that there might be some sufficiently strong teleporters among the enemy who could carry along an unconscious man during one of their tele-jumps. After some deliberation Khrest accepted this possibility as to what really had transpired.

Meanwhile he had got up from the floor and examined the only door leading in or out of this room. The door seemed to be made of solid steel and he couldn't open it. The only furnishings the room contained were a chair and a table.

Khrest sat down on the chair and began to wait. He regretted that it was not his habit to always carry a weapon on him. Among the most effective Arkonide thermo-rayguns there were some small enough to be overlooked with a high degree of probability during a body search.

About one hour after Khrest had awakened the door opened and a man whom Khrest never had seen before snapped at him: 'Come along!'

Khrest didn't bother to get up. He simply raised his eyebrows and inquired: 'Where to?'

The man pointed an automatic at the Arkonide scientist. 'You'll find out in time!' he bellowed angrily.

Khrest stood up and walked past the man and through the door. He found himself now in an adjoining room which was in no way any more comfortable than the first one. A table, a chair; that was all.

They passed into still another room beyond the second one which in addition to the usual meager furnishings also contained some kind of a videophone.

'Take the chair and sit down in front of the screen!' commanded the man, his automatic still pointing at Khrest.

Khrest obeyed. The man remained standing near the door and Khrest was just about to ask him what would happen next when suddenly the v'phone screen lit up. No picture could be seen on it, only a confusion of flickering, jerky, white wavy lines.

At the same moment Khrest felt the peculiar humming pressure in his skull. He reacted instantaneously. Arkonide brains—and in particular as carefully trained a brain as Khrest's—had no difficulty in resisting any kind of telepathic or hypnotic influence.

However, he did understand the meaning of the hypnotic message: *From now on you'll be working for me. I need a man like yourself. I'll show my appreciation for services rendered. You'll become my devoted, loyal servant!*

Khrest recognized at once what confronted him here. The wavy lines on the picture screen were the outflow and amplification of a hypnotic broadcast which would exert its influence on the person regarding the screen.

That meant that Rhodan's assumption had been wrong: the unknown foe possessed not only the powers residing in his own brain but also some mechanical means to produce hypnotic commands even if they initially were still rather inefficient and immature.

An unsympathetic voice began to speak after the hypno-broadcast had been running for almost two minutes. 'Well, I got you after all!'

Khrest didn't bother answering that greeting.

'From now on you'll work for me!' declared the voice.

Khrest decided to lay his cards on the table. 'No, I will not!' he said firmly.

This seemed to puzzle the unknown speaker for a few moments but then he continued: 'Ah.... ! I see ... it didn't work then with you. Never mind for the time being. I already know your personal frequency. Don't think you'll be able to resist me for any length of time—Guard! Take that man away!'

The guard led Khrest back to the room where he had awakened over an hour ago. Khrest sat down at the table and started to think about his situation.

6/ GHOST TROOPS TO THE RESCUE

On his way to the restaurant Nyssen received a call from Rhodan over his micro-telecom, telling him that Rhodan and 20 men had landed northeast of Osaka in order to conduct a search for the unknown enemy's hiding place. Nyssen was requested to supply at once all the data he had gathered in the meantime.

He turned right around and drove back to his hotel. He parked his car in front and took the elevator up to his room.

The first thing he saw on entering his room was Michikai. He was stretched out on the floor with a hole in his forehead. Blood, now dark and dried, had trickled from the wound across his temple onto the wornout rug.

The two men who had brought Michikai to Nyssen's room were flanking the door. Each held a gun in his hand and left no doubt in Nyssen's mind who the next victim might be.

Nyssen was scared; but he regained his composure after a couple of seconds. On the outside, however, he gave the appearance of being close to a nervous breakdown. He mumbled softly a jumbled-up sentence with a distraught air.

His liaison man, who had been ordered by Rhodan to stay at a distance of some 20 miles and be in constant telecommunication with Nyssen, had a great deal of trouble trying to make any sense out of his words.

'... Hotel, Gate of the Heavenly Birds, ... room two, one, one, seven ... two men ... took me prisoner!'

The two intruders were standing about nine feet away from Nyssen. The active part of his microphone had been inserted into the skin of his throat in order to pick up the slightest movements of his larynx. There was a good chance that the two men would not understand what he was murmuring. Nyssen did his best to produce a lot of saliva, letting it drip in a thin thread out of the left corner of his mouth. This made him truly look like a crazed man who had been shocked out of his wits.

One of the men approached. He was grinning. 'What's all the fuss about? We aren't going to harm you!'

'What do you want?' stammered Nyssen.

The man pointed at Michikai's body. 'Deliver this man here and invite you to a come along on a ride.'

'N .. n .. o ... !' protested Nyssen loudly. 'I don't want to!'

'Shut up, you fool! We saw how you finished off that poor guy here, you get it?' And he pointed once more at Michikai. 'You should thank us that we haven't called in the police but've offered to take you along with us instead.'

'Where to?' asked Nyssen, frightened.

'You'll find out in time.—Do you have any weapons?'

'No ... I mean yes, I do!' And he pointed to his left

shoulder. They were bound to find the heavy neutron raygun sooner or later, regardless of whether he told them about it or not.

The man stepped behind him and reached under Nyssen's left armpit. He undid the strap of the gun-holster and with great interest examined the heavy weapon.

'It's O.K. now!' he said after he had finished frisking Nyssen. 'Let's leave!'

His companion opened the door and stepped out in the hallway. Nyssen started to move.

They passed by the desk clerk who didn't notice that anything out of the ordinary was going on. Unchallenged, the two men and Nyssen reached the car that had brought them to the hotel. The driver started the engine while they got in. Nyssen sat on the backseat, the two men on either side of him.

As the car began to move he muttered into the telecom-mike under his breath: 'Driving off!' hoping that his liaison would interpret it correctly.

For the next 30 minutes the car wound its way through the morning traffic jam in the narrow streets of the city. Then they got onto one of the main roads leaving the city and took off at a high speed in a north-easterly direction.

Nyssen had enough time to develop a plan of action. He knew that what mattered mainly now was not to become subjected to the hypnotic influence of the unknown enemy.

The helmet Nyssen had brought along for this purpose from Terrania was lying well-hidden at the bottom of his suitcase back in his hotel room.

There must be some other way to avoid falling victim to the enemy's hypnotic commands.

Such as, for instance, to divert the unknown foe's attention by some incidents which would seem to be more important than hypnotizing his new prisoner.

Inside the entire area of the circle whose position Rhodan had determined with the help of Tako Kakuta's tele-jump data, there were only three buildings. One was a dilapidated barn which didn't give the impression it would have a basement. The other two were country villas built in a typical Japanese style.

Rhodan had landed in this territory together with 20 men during the early hours of the morning. Their transporter had taken off immediately after discharging its cargo and passengers.

Rhodan and his men were dressed in special Arkonide transport suits. They were equipped with microgenerators which produced antigravity, deflector and protective fields.

It had caused no trouble for Rhodan and his men to spend the better part of the morning hidden in a little nearby forest.

At first Nyssen's abduction had been an unpleasant surprise. But just as swiftly as the kidnapped major, Rhodan also recognized the opportunity which this event could offer. All along the ride with his two abductors, Nyssen kept up a running commentary describing the direction the car was taking, so that in the end Rhodan no longer had any doubt which of the two country villas was his real goal.

Rhodan also understood Nyssen's plan to divert the attention of the unknown, who was awaiting the arrival of his latest prisoner, in such a manner as to afford Nyssen a free hand for at least the first half hour after arriving at his place of incarceration.

No contact could be established with Khrest. The Arkonide scientist had never accepted the fact that it might come in handy under certain circumstances to have a micro-telecom implanted in his skin. Rhodan was firmly convinced however that by now Khrest surely had changed his mind.

The mutant master stared with unbelieving eyes at the image showing on the picture screen of his warning and surveillance installation.

A stranger!

He was standing in the small interior courtyard which was surrounded by the walls of the square building complex of his farm house. The stranger was wearing a suit of a type never before encountered by Monterny. The man held a short-barrelled, thick weapon in his hand.

Monterny noticed that the man kept looking around as if searching for something.

One second later he had vanished again.

But an instant afterwards he reappeared at another place.

No! This wasn't the same man. He was smaller than the first stranger and had broader shoulders!

Monterny felt his hands starting to tremble uncontrollably.

Two men had managed to pass unnoticed through

the outer defense perimeter and to penetrate into the interior courtyard and they could make themselves invisible at will!

Monterny gave the alarm signal.

The two men however had vanished meanwhile and did not reappear for the time being.

It happened exactly the way Nyssen had hoped it would. The two men led him into the villa through a side entrance. There he was told to wait. One of his guards remained with him while the other walked down a corridor and disappeared in one of the rooms.

When he reappeared one minute later he had looked plainly disgusted.

'He can't be bothered just now!' he yelled to the other guard. 'Take him downstairs!'

An elevator took Nyssen and his captor into the basement. He was locked in a room which Nyssen believed he recognized as the one Kakuta had described. Of course Nyssen couldn't know that there were exactly 30 similar rooms in the basement of this farmhouse.

Nyssen sat down on the only chair in the room, planted his elbows on the table and rested his bowed head in his hands. He pretended to be a desperate man for the benefit of the TV spy system which he assumed to be built into the walls.

In reality he was putting the finishing touches to his plan, remaining as cool as a cucumber on the inside. There was one factor that worried him: He had to consider some unknown quantity in his calculations —the alertness of his opponent.

His plan could succeed only if everybody in this house—including every single man on guard duty—would be totally distracted from their duties by the events taking place in the vicinity and on the grounds proper of the villa.

New strangers made their appearance, all dressed in the same strange-looking suits, all equipped with the same ability to render themselves invisible.

Monterny had no doubt that they had penetrated the interior courtyard by arriving through the air.

For a few minutes he was under the impression that the intruders had come to free his prisoners. This impression changed very soon when he discovered one of the strangers for a fraction of a second on the roof of his villa. He had appeared right next to the big antenna used for beaming out the hypno-broadcasts.

This discovery greatly alarmed the mutant master. He had a force of 30 guards at his disposal for the protection of his base. He positioned 15 men on the roof to protect his antenna. Ten other guards were patrolling the grounds around the villa. They were given orders to shoot on sight at anything moving through the air in the vicinity of the base.

Having thus done everything he could for the defense of his domain, Monterny prepared for a swift flight. He had arrived at the conclusion that he was practically sitting in a trap. Supposing Rhodan—and the mutant master was fully convinced that these invisible people must be Rhodan's men—did not place such great a value on the prisoners as he Monterny first believed he would—then Rhodan might blow up this base at any moment by his ghost troops.

Although Monterny quickly changed his opinion about an impending explosion, he acted as if he still believed in it.

He was a very cautious man who always carefully planned ahead. Underneath the house, starting from a cellar to which he was the only person to have access, he had built an underground passage which ran for $\frac{3}{4}$ of a mile underground and then emerged again at the surface.

Three-quarters of a mile should be enough, estimated Monterny, to remove himself to a safe distance from Rhodan's range of action.

Exactly one hour after his imprisonment began, Nyssen started banging his fists against the door. He kept this up for a quarter of an hour. Then he heard shuffling steps approach his room.

He continued pounding on his door until it started to open. This was the moment when he stepped quickly aside and ducked.

The guard held the pistol in his hand ready to shoot. But Nyssen came from another direction than the one in which the man thought the prisoner was standing.

A Karate-chop caught the guard in exactly the right spot. He screamed in pain, dropped his weapon and whirled around. But he was slow in comparison to Nyssen. Another chop and the guard slumped quickly to the ground.

He was knocked out for one minute. In the meantime Nyssen had grabbed his weapon and convinced himself that the area outside and all along the corridor was clear.

'You listen to me!' he snapped at the guard. 'Listen carefully! I'm in a bad spot here. I *need* you to get out. I don't want to get caught again. I'll shoot you cold if you do anything I don't like. Anything! Understand?'

The man was a Japanese. He hastily nodded his head to express his agreement. Nyssen was certain that the man was subject to only a very mild post hypnotic suggestion now. If everything was going the way Nyssen had planned then the unknown leader of this group must be too preoccupied otherwise at the moment to be able to keep an eye on each and every one of his men.

In any case, the guard's fear of death seemed to outweigh the post-hypnotic command. The Japanese seemed quite meek now.

'There's another prisoner down here,' declared Nyssen. 'Where is he kept?'

The guard pointed down the hall.

'How many guards are there down here altogether?'
'Five.'

'Lead me to the other prisoner but make sure we don't run into any of your colleagues!'

The Japanese led Nyssen for a few minutes in a criss-cross pattern through the basement. Twice they heard some strange voices from afar but they didn't meet anybody.

Then they found Khrest.

The Arkonide scientist needed a little while to

adjust to the new situation. Nyssen had some difficulty in convincing him what the next step in his plan was going to be.

'We're far from safe yet!' declared Nyssen with determination. 'The unknown enemy still has a firm grip on his base. We must get back the neutron ray-gun they've taken away from me!'

Finally Khrest began to see the light. He agreed then to everything Nyssen proposed. Such as opening his door and shouting at the top of his voice. His guard came running down the corridor, astonished at Khrest's unusual behavior, and was hit over the head from behind by Nyssen. The guard collapsed on the floor without resistance.

They crept stealthily past the other three guards. They reached the elevator. Khrest remained at the entrance to stand guard, armed with the weapon they had captured, while Nyssen and the Japanese guard rode up to the ground floor. The guard gave Khrest the information where he might find the neutron ray-gun. It was in the same room where one of his guards had disappeared for a minute shortly after their arrival at the base.

Taking a calculated risk Nyssen stormed into the room, which fortunately for him was empty now since all the base personnel had been deployed elsewhere. He quickly seized his gun and both men then returned to the basement. There he made some complicated manipulations of the weapon, following Khrest's instructions. Then he placed the weapon at a spot he judged to be both safe and effective for his future plans.

And finally he got in touch with Perry Rhodan.

A few minutes afterwards, Rhodan's men proceeded to attack the villa from two sides. They remained clearly visible in the open. The attack from the west began two minutes earlier than from the south. This had the result that the southern side of the house was nearly unguarded for this brief time span.

Khrest and Nyssen made good use of this time. They made a hundred yard dash, running straight into the arms of Rhodan's advancing men.

Rhodan was informed of Khrest's and Nyssen's rescue. At once he ordered the attack to be stopped. One of his men, armed with a microphone and a loud-speaker, penetrated into the interior courtyard of the villa and broadcast an announcement which could be clearly heard by everybody, even the guards down in the cellars: 'Clear these premises immediately! You have five minutes to get out! Then a bomb will be detonated which will annihilate all life within a radius of 100 yards.'

Naturally, the effect of this warning was practically nil. Everyone in the farmhouse believed it to be a trick. The men tried to ask Monterny for advice but he was unavailable.

The men decided then to wait and after the five minutes had passed without anything untoward happening, all began to triumph.

However neutron rays can be neither seen nor heard nor smelled. Not even neutron flows of 10^{17} neutrons per 0.155 square inch per second.

That the bomb actually had exploded was not

noticed by Monterny's men until their skin suddenly turned red and started to hurt. Within a few seconds they lost their eyesight. In sheer panic the blind men started racing through the corridors, trying to get out of the house. But by then it was too late.

Only two guards who had obeyed the evacuation order escaped the catastrophe. They surrendered to Rhodan's men.

As far as the Japanese were concerned they became officially alerted about the strange events that had taken place at the northern end of the main road leading out of Osaka when somebody noticed astonishingly high radioactivity in that area.

That was five hours after Nyssen had detonated the bomb. In the meantime, Rhodan, the two freed men, the two prisoners they had taken and Rhodan's expeditionary force had all left the country. In addition they brought back to Terrania all the experiences they had gathered during their search of the unknown enemy's base.

This conference took place two days later. Rhodan had assembled his friends in order to tell them of the findings of his latest mission.

'We haven't gained as much as we hoped we would,' stated Rhodan in a serious tone. 'As far as we have been able to ascertain from both our prisoners and the owner of the printshop whom we also seized in the meantime, the most important person we wanted to capture has escaped. None of our prisoners has ever seen this dangerous stranger face to face, not directly in person nor on the videoscreen. There was only one confidante in that house with whom he had direct personal contact. But this man was found among the dead in the villa. And from a dead man you can't learn anything.

'We've found the underground passage through which the man made his escape. But we have lost any further trace of him.

'The few records we found in the base give no hints about his plans, activities and potential as an opponent. Even if we were to assume that those people in his Japanese base who by their own obstinacy met their death, constituted his entire crew, it wouldn't present any difficulty for this man to recruit new followers. He has his own special means, very effective and very despicable. Therefore we must not let ourselves be lulled into a false sense of security by the hope that this war is over. For the time being we haven't even been able to find the scientists that were kidnapped from Terrania.

'There are three things we have discovered so far:

'Besides his actual co-worker team, at present no longer in existence, the unknown enemy has at his disposal an undetermined number of middlemen. This brought death to Michikai, the Japanese chap working for Nyssen, and also almost cost Nyssen's life as well.

'Secondly we know the process by which the unknown foe's mechanized-hypnotic influence is being transmitted. Whenever he gets in touch with his people via v'phone, the most important message is not the verbal part but the wave pattern seen on the screen. It's questionable however whether he'll continue this method of communication once he realizes that we have found out about it.

'The third thing we know is that the destruction of the enemy's base near Osaka must have been felt by him as a bitter reverse. As little as we might have actually accomplished, we at least foiled one of his plans. It is not unlikely that this will cause him to lose his nerve and that he might make a few mistakes during the next days which hopefully will lead us closer to wherever he is hiding now.'

Perry Rhodan, that same evening at 8 o'clock, personally accompanied Betty Toufry to the aircraft which was to fly her to New York. He spoke softly but urgently to the little mutant, who listened with utmost attention.

'There will be many things you won't understand about this mission, Betty. What we hope to accomplish depends to some extent on our success in keeping the General Cosmic Company alive. You're going to New York now to protect Mr. Adams from all enemies who will try to get close to him unnoticed.

'You'll have to keep your eyes and ears and all your *other* senses wide open, Betty!'

The tiny Ms. Toufry halted her pace for a moment and gazed intently into Rhodan's eyes. 'I promise to be on the alert at all times,' she said solemnly. A short while later she was on her way to New York.

And that same evening Captain Barina reported to Rhodan from Salt Lake City that he still hadn't found any trace of Richman's murderer. 'If I hadn't seen his body with my own eyes I wouldn't believe someone actually killed him. It's the perfect crime—not a trace ... nothing at all!'

Rhodan pondered the problem a moment, realized there were others more pressing, decided to abandon the search for Richman's murderer, told Barina so and switched off.

At this point Thora entered Rhodan's room. The door closed quietly behind her and she remained very still as she observed Perry sitting lost in thought. He sat staring at the colorful little lights of the big telecom switchboard and at first she thought he hadn't noticed her entry. But presently, without looking directly at her, he said: 'There's so much work ahead of us, Thora. Do you realize that?'

Thora came closer. 'Yes, I've a pretty good idea.'

Perry now directed his gaze at the comely Arkonide. 'There's one problem in particular for which we haven't a hint of an answer yet.'

Thora thought she knew the one he meant. 'The explosion in block G—?'

'Exactly. We can imagine how the destroyers were removed: one teleporter of the caliber of the one who abducted Khrest could do it. One by one—or maybe even both at the same time—he could teleport his accomplices to Terrania to materialize inside the command center of the destroyers. The rest would be easy from then on.

'But how someone could manage to cause a nuclear explosion in a huge assembly plant which didn't contain even a milligram of nuclear explosives—well, that's a mystery of the first order.'

123

Perry paused briefly.

Thora broke the silence with a question that for her was an unprecedented admission of admiration: 'Do you really think that a man like you will remain in the dark for long?'

Perry was shocked. He looked at the platinum-haired enigmatic alien intently, searching her beautiful face for a sign of derision—but of mockery there was not a trace.

The planets threatened to reverse their orbits.

The sun to go nova.

The moon to fall.

Plainly, incontrovertibly, incredibly, *Thora had paid Perry a compliment!*

Did the future hold any greater surprises?

BEFORE THE GOLDEN AGE 1

Isaac Asimov

For many s.f. addicts the Golden Age began in 1938 when John Campbell became editor of Astounding Stories. For Isaac Asimov, the formative and most memorable period came in the decade before the Golden Age – the 1930s. It is to the writers of this generation that BEFORE THE GOLDEN AGE is dedicated.

Some – Jack Williamson, Murray Leinster, Stanley Weinbaum and Asimov himself – have remained famous to this day. Others such as Neil Jones, S. P. Meek and Charles Tanner, have been deservedly rescued from oblivion.

BEFORE THE GOLDEN AGE was originally published in the United States in a single mammoth volume of almost 1,200 pages. The British paperback edition will appear in four books, the first of which covers the years 1930 to 1933.

BEFORE THE GOLDEN AGE 3

Isaac Asimov

In this third volume, Isaac Asimov has selected a feast of rousing tales such as BORN BY THE SUN by Jack Williamson, with its marvellous vision of the solar system as a giant incubator; Murray Leinster's story of parallel time-tracks SIDEWISE IN TIME; and Raymond Z. Gallin's OLD FAITHFUL which features one of science fiction's most memorable aliens – Number 774.

'Sheer nostalgic delight ... stories by authors long-forgotten mingle with those by ones who are well-known, and still writing. A goldmine for anyone interested in the evolution of s.f.'
Sunday Times

'Contains some of the very best s.f. from the Thirties ... emphatically value for money.'
Evening Standard

A MIDSUMMER TEMPEST

Poul Anderson

'The best writing he's done in years ... his language is superb. Worth buying for your permanent collection.'
– *The Alien Critic*

Somewhere, spinning through another universe, is an Earth where a twist of fate, a revolution and a few early inventions have made a world quite unlike our own.

It is a world where Cavaliers and Puritans battle with the aid of observation balloons and steam trains; where Oberon and Titania join forces with King Arthur to resist the Industrial Revolution; and where the future meshes with the past in the shape of Valeria, time traveller from New York.

PROTECTOR

Larry Niven

Phssthpok the Pak had been travelling for most of his 32,000 years – his mission, to save, develop and protect the group of pak breeders sent out into space some 2½ million years before ...

Brennan was a Belter, the product of a fiercely independent, somewhat anarchic society living in, on and around an outer asteroid belt. The Belters were rebels one and all, and Brennan was a Smuggler. The Belt worlds had been tracking the pak ship for days – Brennan figured to meet that ship first ...

He was never seen again – at least not in the form of homo sapiens.

Larry Niven is the author of RINGWORLD which won both the Hugo and Nebula awards for the best s.f. novel of the year.

THE FLIGHT OF THE HORSE

Larry Niven

These are the stories of Svetz the harassed Time Retrieval Expert and of the mind-bending difficulties created when his Department supplies him with inadequate information....

Here too are his strange adventures with horses, unicorns, ostriches, rocs and other unlikely fauna, both extinct and as yet unborn ... In THE FLIGHT OF THE HORSE, Larry Niven has written a collection of science fiction stories which combine fantasy and mainstream s.f. with superb story telling.